ANNIE DALTON

THE
RULES
⬧OF
MAGIC

ALSO BY ANNIE DALTON

The Afterdark Princess
The Dream Snatcher
The Midnight Museum

For younger readers

The Real Tilly Beany
Tilly Beany and the Best Friend Machine
Tilly Beany Saves the World

ANNIE DALTON

THE RULES OF MAGIC

EGMONT

EGMONT

We bring stories to life

First published in Great Britain 2004
by Mammoth, an imprint of Egmont Children's Books Ltd
a division of Egmont Holding Limited
239 Kensington High Street, London W8 6SA

Text copyright © 2004 Annie Dalton
Cover photograph © 2004 Getty Images

The moral rights of the author has been asserted

ISBN 1 4052 0058 8

1 3 5 7 9 10 8 6 4 2

A CIP catalogue record for this title is available from the British Library

Typeset by Avon DataSet Ltd, Bidford on Avon, Warwickshire
Printed and bound in Great Britain by CPI Group

With awe and gratitude to Miriam Hodgson most intuitive, also most exacting of editors. You always know how to make an author raise her game!

Also loving thanks to Maria, who got me started by telling me about the thirteenth floor; to Reuben, who showed me how it feels to pull down the sounds; and to Anna, Philipp, Sophie and Izzie, for reminding me what matters.

PROLOGUE

'Never give your power away. People take advantage.'
Dino Skerakis

SOMETHING happened last night. Now I can't get it out of my head.

I keep picturing myself eavesdropping in the dark, while my father poured out his confession, and I get gripped by this cold panic. My head starts swimming and I can't breathe and I don't seem to know what's real.

It'll soon be light, light as it ever gets this time of year. I can almost make out the misty shapes of tower blocks. Somewhere down there in the city, amongst rotting warehouses and tarted-up riverside apartments, is Mortagaine House.

That's where it happened, if you believe Dad. I don't. I refuse to believe all that garbage he was spouting last night. Just because those stories scared me

1

rigid when I was younger doesn't mean they're true. They were never even intended for adults. OK, we were all hooked on them when we were younger. We'd sneak into that old boarded-up house after school and listen to Tina Tillotson, completely transfixed.

Tina can't have been more than six months older than we were, but she had this freaky voice which made her sound like some wise old oracle.

Her storytelling sessions always started the same way.

'Grown-ups think Mortagaine House is built out of bricks like normal buildings. It isn't. They believe it was built by human beings. It wasn't. I'm going to tell you what really happened. One night when the city was sleeping . . .'

But that's when we were *nine*! So Mortagaine House is hideous. Loads of old buildings are hideous. They can't *all* be sites for supernatural goings-on.

I never understood why Dad moved back there after he and Mum split up. People tend to move to Mortagaine House because they're broke and just starting out, or more usually because the bottom just dropped out of their world.

My parents were in the first category. Apart from

2

their lack of money, everything in their world was rosy. They were still in love, and had the touching belief that everything would work out.

The only cloud on their horizon was that Mum couldn't have kids. Even this they got around by deciding to adopt. Only a few days after they got me their fortunes dramatically improved and they were able to move into a gorgeous house in St Clements. Dad used to say I brought them good luck.

It's humiliating to think how easily I swallowed this cheesy explanation. I guess it fitted in with the 'chosen child' scenario my parents loved to tell me when I was little.

I was a gorgeous baby, if I say it myself: the perfect colour match for my Irish dad and Jamaican mum. 'That's one magic little princess you got there!' a neighbour cooed to my dad, two days after they brought me home. It's the kind of thing people say to new fathers.

But my father is a gambling man and he practically went into orbit. A horse called Magic Princess was running in the 2.30 that afternoon.

'I'd been waiting for a sign,' he'd tell me in that silky storytelling voice he puts on. 'And here it was!'

Dad raced down to the bookies and put all the money they had in the world on this total outsider. Magic Princess won by two lengths, at a stupendous hundred to one.

'How did you know, Daddy?' I'd say in awe. 'How did you *know* Magic Princess would win?'

Dad always gave the same answer. 'You told me.'

'But babies can't talk!'

'You told me in here.' Dad would tap his forehead. 'You were my magic princess. Magic little Princess Bee.'

But that's not the version he was telling as I listened on the stairs.

'I had to do it, Claudette,' he told Mum drunkenly. 'I wanted us all to live happily ever after like people in a fairy tale . . .'

My eyes are hot and gritty from lack of sleep. I lean my face against the ice-cold glass of the window, until my skin goes pleasantly numb. Where did Dad get the idea fairy tales were happy? All those defenceless children at the mercy of selfish adults.

All those evil bargains, something whispers.

Horror rushes through me like a freezing wind. I keep telling myself that my father simply isn't capable

4

of doing anything so cruel, but it's like I've started falling, and now I can't stop. I'm literally gripping on to the window frame just to feel something solid.

If only there was someone I could tell.

Oh, I've got friends, but they don't know me. I'm Bee Molloy, the girl all the other girls secretly want to be. How can I tell them my picture-perfect life just blew apart?

If only I hadn't heard my father hammering on our front door; if only, if *only* I hadn't let him in. I hadn't heard from him in months. It was past midnight and I was all alone downstairs. It could have been some crazed psycho out there. It's almost like I had a sixth sense. I flew downstairs to the hall, dragged back both bolts and flung open the door.

For a moment I wasn't sure this was actually my dad. The man on the step hadn't changed his clothes for days. Booze fumes floated off him in waves.

'Daddy? Are you *nuts?*' I hissed. 'It's really late.'

His voice was blurry with alcohol. 'I need to talk to your mother! I've done something terrible, Bee.'

Lights were going on in the houses on either side. 'Keep it down!' someone shouted. 'People are trying to sleep!'

I linked my arm through his and helped him over the step. I could feel a clammy heat rising through his sleeve, as if he was going down with flu.

'A terrible terrible thing,' he repeated thickly. 'The worst thing any man could do.' My father stumbled into the hall lampshade on the way in, sending weird shadows flitting over the walls. He grabbed my hand. 'Tell Claudette I need to talk to her.' He was gripping so hard it hurt.

I pulled away. 'I'm not waking Mum on some whim. She's tired out!'

'Bee, I'm begging you. It's a matter of life and death.'

I made my voice calm and reasonable, like Mum sounds when she's talking a client out of quitting rehab.

'Not a good idea,' I said. 'Mum's had a rough day and you're not in great shape yourself. Why not come back when you're both feeling –'

I heard a door open on the top floor. Mum came stumbling downstairs in her pyjamas, all puffy with sleep. She stared at us, totally appalled. 'Are you out of your minds?'

My father lunged to embrace her, but she shoved him off.

'No, you don't, James Molloy. Not in the state you're in.'

'Mum, I think Dad's ill!'

'Funny illness,' she said sharply. 'Smells like whiskey.'

'God, you're so heartless!' I told her.

'I had to come, Claudette. I didn't know where else to go.' Dad sounded like a scared little kid.

'Lord have mercy,' my mother said in a resigned voice. 'You always did know which strings to pull. OK, come on up. Make your old man some coffee, Bees. Strong, black, plenty of sugar. Then off to bed.'

I obeyed in a way that showed I did not appreciate being bossed about like an eight-year-old child, making a point of giving my father a warm hug on the way out. When Mum whisks me offstage like this, it's a sign she and Dad are going to fight, over maintenance payments usually. But so far as I'm concerned, what affects Dad affects me, so I shut the living-room door, tiptoed halfway up the stairs and sat straining my ears in the dark.

'Where's your toy boy?' I heard Dad say bitterly. 'Catching up on his beauty sleep upstairs, I suppose?'

Dad dislikes Mum's boyfriend as much as I do, and

no wonder. The jerk is inferior to my father in every way. When Victor Waverley walks through our door, I walk straight out. He hasn't even got a normal job, just does youth work plus supply teaching on the side. There's no shortage of schools in this city, luckily. If he ever showed up at mine I'd die of shame.

'Victor never stays over, you know that,' Mum says. 'Now maybe you'll tell me why you felt you had to wake the whole street?'

Dad didn't even mention money, to my relief, just launched into a confused story about his latest girlfriend.

Sadie is literally young enough to be my big sister. Mum and I call her the Flower Child. She's a complete ditz. According to my father the first eighteen months of their relationship were idyllic. Unfortunately Sadie got it into her head that they needed a baby. 'I told her she was too young for such a big responsibility. "At least practise on a kitten first," I told her. "You can give it away if things don't work out." And I kept telling and telling her I wasn't able father material,' he added sheepishly.

Sadie had finally worn Dad down. After a couple of setbacks, she was now hugely, unstoppably

8

pregnant. The girl had the nerve to call me up one Saturday while she was skipping around department stores, picking out dinky sleep-suits and cot mobiles. She said she thought I might like to come and help her choose a crib! I'm like, 'Why? This kid has nothing whatsoever to do with me!'

Despite initial misgivings, Dad admitted that when Sadie told him she was having their child, he was overwhelmed with joy. 'It felt as if I'd been given a second chance, Claudette. Maybe I'd do it better second time around.'

I felt a funny ache inside. What was I then, Dad? A rehearsal?

Sofa springs twanged. I could hear Dad pacing. 'Then I started having these – I suppose you'd have to call them, uh, visions.'

The house was suddenly silent. I could hear my heart thudding in my ears.

'I see,' Mum said in her calm, I've-heard-everything, social worker voice. 'You don't think maybe your druggy youth is catching up with you?'

Dad gave a strained laugh. 'Oh how I wish that's all it was!'

'You're saying this is *worse* than fried brain cells?'

'Much, much worse. At first they came when I was drifting off to sleep. Now I'm getting them in broad daylight. Today I actually had to pull over on to the hard shoulder. It's a miracle I didn't crash the car.'

'Jimmie, they could still be flashbacks.'

I heard a mug clatter to the table.

'Jesus, Mary and Joseph!' Dad exploded. 'It was sixteen *years* ago, Claudette! I was young and foolish. How was I to know that one reckless impulse would come back to haunt me after all this time?'

My mind was whirling with lurid storylines by this time. Had Dad cheated on Mum while they were married? Did he have a secret love child somewhere? Was someone blackmailing him?

'Why don't you stop going all round the houses and tell me what's really worrying you? It's not as if you can shock me. Social workers are shockproof. Also permanently tired. By morning I'll have forgotten everything you told me.'

'Claudette, I'd love to believe it was that simple –'

'Believe it,' Mum said wearily. 'Just get it off your chest and we can all get some sleep.'

For a long time all I heard was Dad's ragged breathing.

'All right,' he said slowly. 'But if I tell you, you've to promise you'll never tell Bee.'

I sat up bolt upright in the dark. I should have gone to bed right then. But something kept me glued on the stairs.

So now I know. It was me.

I'm the reason my father was as drunk as a skunk, babbling about terrifying visions. I'm the one who ruined his last chance of happiness. It's all because of me.

My mother's alarm clock goes off on the other side of the wall.

We take turns to use the bathroom, passing on the landing without a word. Mum and I discovered that the best way to avoid rows in the morning is not to talk.

Downstairs, Mum silently catches up on paperwork, sipping her sacred Blue Mountain coffee. She hasn't set foot in Jamaica since she was six years old. Since Auntie Blossom died, Mum doesn't have a single Jamaican relative, yet she still has this big rootsy thing going on, even insists on twisting her hair into little locks. She used to try to get me all fired up about Jamaica too, then I pointed out that neither of us has the first clue where my original birth parents came from, and she finally got the message.

I put up the ironing board and set the iron on 'steam'.

'So have you got some groovy Halloween activities lined up?' the radio DJ witters to a caller. 'Are you into spooks and magic spells?'

I'm not listening, I'm not even thinking, but as I smooth out the crinkles in my new white top, the radio voices blur and I drift into a memory of Halloween.

Hollowed-out pumpkins glow in the window of the local taverna. Dino, the owner's son, and I are playing house under a table, telling spooky stories, shivering with terror that is nearly as delicious as the pastries Dino's aunt smuggles to us under the tablecloth.

Above our heads, my parents flirt over their meal. 'Jimmie, you're crazy!' Mum keeps saying, making 'crazy' sound like a sexy endearment.

I like Dino. I like him a lot. I like how he doesn't smile just because he's supposed to. I haven't yet heard the expression 'soulmates'. I just know that when I'm with this boy, the world has more colours.

Inside our starched tablecloth tent, Dino tells me an electrifying secret. 'We used to know how to do magic,' he whispers into my ear.

'Really?'

'Yes. But I can't remember the rules. Can you?'

I consider this solemnly. 'I might remember some.'

The iron lets out a jet of steam. Nothing turns out the way you think. Who'd have guessed that sweet six year old would grow into a stubble-headed moron in basketball boots?

I go upstairs, dress and put on make-up. I tell myself I can't feel the shattered-glass feeling in my chest. If I can't feel it, maybe it isn't there.

Sometimes we didn't even have to speak. One time, Dino sang a tune out loud that I'd been humming privately inside my head.

The memory feels so close that I shut my eyes and beam a message through time.

I'm scared, Dino, I whisper to him in my mind. *Help me.*

Then I pick up my mascara wand and carry on turning myself into the perfectly groomed teenager everyone knows as Bee Molloy.

CHAPTER ONE

'YO! Skerakis!'

A paper missile hits me under my ear. I come out of my Friday afternoon slump to see my oldest mate pulling mad faces. 'Still on for tonight?' Despite the jokey tone I know Marlon's embarrassed.

'Yeah, I'm coming. Why wouldn't I be?'

There's no way I'm letting anyone at this school know how completely my family has come unhinged, not even my best mate.

I give an incredulous laugh, showing him just how far off-track he is. 'We just moved house, man! No reason to pass up a chance to party with the don.'

Marlon loves it when anyone refers to him as a gangster, almost as much as he hates it when life gets too heavy.

He grins with obvious relief. 'I told Jude we could count on you!'

They drag their chairs over and we discuss our plans

for the night. As usual we wind up agreeing to go to Chaos. We keep saying we'll check out Urban Legends, but we never do.

Bee Molloy and her mates are chatting at the next table. Roshelle is playing them a tune on her minidisc player: an old Mimi Rousseau track, which some new girl band recently remixed with a hip hop beat. Roshelle turns up the volume until the vibes judder pleasurably up my spine.

My dad jokes that we're a generation of mutants. We can't even eat like civilised people. We graze on the move or bolt junk food in front of the TV. And we never just watch one programme from start to finish, we surf from one channel to another; at the same time we're texting our mates, checking emails and football scores and moving, always moving to heavy house or hip hop beats inside our heads.

'It's called evolution, Dad,' I tell him. 'We're adapting to deal with pressures your lot never dreamed of. It's a dangerous world. You've got to be on it or you won't survive.'

Like, at this moment it looks as if I'm just sitting flexing with my mates, but I'm actually hyper-aware of everything that's going on in this room. Take Leo currently exploiting the teacher's absence to showcase his wide range of 'sweeties' to a couple of would-be clients. Then there's Jay, our class nutter. I didn't hear what he just said to Tariq, but I don't like the vibes. Jay's last fit of classroom rage ended with flying chairs. And Bee Molloy is sitting too close for my peace of mind.

No one knows why our teacher didn't turn up to teach general studies and, to be honest, no one cares. General studies isn't even a real subject, plus we're all gradually winding down for the weekend.

Outside, the heavy rain is battering the windows. A leaf flattens itself against the glass then whirls away.

'Can you believe this weather?' Persia pulls her fluffy wraparound top more tightly around her. She's the kind of girl who constantly draws attention to her female assets. Most boys think she's seriously hot. I avoid her like the plague. Outside old movies, any girl who tries to pull that helpless sex-kitten routine is either disturbingly damaged, playing games or plain nuts; or, in Persia's case, a scary combination of all three.

'It's always like this at Halloween,' says Roshelle.

Bee makes a sound that could be agreement but I know she's miles away. This morning she barged right into me in the corridor. When she realised it was me, she literally changed colour, her bag slipped out of her hands and all her stuff flew everywhere.

'Am I *that* ugly?' I teased.

She just went on staring open-mouthed, as if she'd seen a ghost. I was going to help her pick up her gear, but all her mates crowded round protectively, so I left them to it.

I've known Bee Molloy for pure time, right back to when we were little rug rats. Her parents used to bring her into Dad's taverna. That was before we all moved up to high school, and Bee got reincarnated as the queen of style. You could talk to her back then; now she scarcely gives me the time of day.

Yet I can't help feeling there's some weird little connection. This is not something I'd admit to my mates. They'd assume I just want to get into her pants, which would obviously be a plus, but it's more than teenage lust. It's something I can't describe, even to myself.

I sneak another glance in Bee's direction. Something is definitely different, disturbingly so, but what? Same understated casuals. No bizarre facial piercings. Nope, I give up.

CRASH! Madman Jay is on his feet, breathing hard.

I'm on it in a flash. I jump up and hurl myself between him and Bee.

A tall black guy in a suit and horn-rims strolls in and dumps his briefcase on the teacher's desk.

Everyone moves like lightning. Leo spirits his supplies out of sight. Roshelle kills the music. Jay backs off, and I rapidly reverse into my seat.

My heart is hammering against my ribs, but the guy doesn't seem to notice anything unusual. 'Apologies for being so late,' he grins. 'The secretary sent me to the wrong end of the school.'

I don't try to hide my disgust. 'Oh, give me a break!'

It's not just the bad suit, or even his shiny little glasses. This supply teacher is the worst kind of phoney. It's written all over him.

'My name is Mr Waverley.' He grabs a lump of chalk and energetically scribbles his name on the board in case the moronic inner-city teenagers have forgotten it already. 'Perhaps you can tell me what you've been doing with Miss Bartlett?'

'Easy,' jeers someone. 'Nothing.'

'We did,' Persia objects. 'We did Greek myths and legends. It *was* Greeks, wasn't it, Dino?' she asks doubtfully.

Everyone howls. Just what I need. More Greek jokes. Because of my ethnic background, Miss Bartlett has appointed me class expert on ancient Greek culture. 'Isn't that so, Dino?' she goes. 'What do you think, Dino?' When I've never even *been* to the Land of freaking Heroes.

Waverley beams at Persia, as if she's given him the opening he needs. 'Which myths have you guys covered so far?'

The way he talks, in a toned-down street style, would be genuinely surprising if it was the real thing, but it's more likely he's faking it, trying to be one of us.

Persia looks trapped. 'Erm, I think there was a tree which turned into a girl. No, wait! The girl turned into a tree!'

She pulls agonised faces, wanting her mates to help her out. Bee gives a stony-faced shrug, and I feel a little buzz of satisfaction. Bee's taken against the new supply teacher too.

Waverley is pacing, still doing the phoney street voice. 'No disrespect to Miss Bartlett. But I'd like to bring her myths and legends idea up to date. Make it more relevant to the twenty-first century.'

'Ooh, I know!' I suggest. 'We could write a rap musical!'

My mates hoot with laughter.

Waverley just goes on making his pitch. 'I'm not sure we're so radically different from the people who told those myths in ancient times. We still love to hear about heroes saving the world, but we rent our stories from Blockbuster instead of telling them around the fire.'

Marlon and I roll our eyes. We've seen his type a million times. They come into our school and immediately they're starring in *Dangerous Minds*. They don't know the first thing about us and they don't intend to find out. A pure power trip, that's all it is.

Waverley is scribbling again. He steps back, and I see the words 'Urban Legends' written neatly on the board. 'Anyone know this phrase?'

Marlon grins. 'Sure, it's meant to be a kicking club.'

'You should try it,' suggests Leo. 'Take the old suit for an airing. Give the moths a treat.'

Waverley raises an eyebrow. 'Thanks for the tip. But I was hoping one of you would define the phenomenon for me.'

'This is beyond pointless,' I say loudly. 'Miss Bartlett will be back next week, getting all overexcited about Zeus or whatever.'

He ignores me, calmly underlining the first word

on the board. 'Let's break it up. We'll take "urban" first. Anyone?'

'It means like towns, cities,' says a boy who only joined our class last week.

Mr Waverley gestures with his chalk. 'As opposed to?'

'The country?' says the new kid hopefully.

'And legends?' Waverley prompts.

I let my head fall forward on to the desk. Could this be any more painful?

There's a faint rustling sound. 'Perhaps I can help you, Victor?'

Waverley looks genuinely thrown, as if he's only just noticed Bee Molloy sitting at the back of the class. Making a lightning recovery, he says, 'By all means.'

She smiles, but it's not a friendly smile.

'Urban legends are sensational stories which express deep-seated anxieties about the pressures of modern life,' she reels off in a cold voice. 'Typically, the person recounting the legend claims to have a friend of a friend, or a distant family member to whom the bizarre event really happened. Yet no one can ever totally pinpoint how this particular story got into circulation. This makes it seem as if urban legends have a genuinely supernatural origin, rather like the legends of ancient times.'

Bee gives the teacher a final cool stare and sits back. Her friends eye her in alarm as if her head might suddenly swivel through 360 degrees.

I am now officially intrigued. Like most girls at my school, Bee Molloy keeps her intelligence well under wraps. There's any number of ways she could have annoyed Waverley but she's deliberately challenged him on his own territory. She *hates* this guy, and she doesn't care who knows it.

Waverley totally doesn't seem to notice Bee has just declared war. 'But *why* are these stories so sensational, that's the question.' He scans the class hopefully.

I put up my hand. 'Sir? I have a theory about that, sir.'

He falls for it. 'Please, let's hear it.'

'Our generation has been exposed to so much sex, violence and horror that we're virtually shockproof,' I tell him airily. 'Urban legends have to be outrageous. It's the only way to penetrate our armour of impervious teen sophistication.'

Bee hastily looks down, trying not to laugh.

'Is your name really Victor?' Ruby calls out.

'Actually it is,' he admits sheepishly.

Kids experiment with this name in various tones:

22

posh, sexy, pleading. Waverley patiently rides this out until they get bored.

'So has anyone come across any particularly outrageous urban legends?' he inquires.

Jay perks up. 'Like that rumour about those tattoos?'

'He said urban *legends*, fool, not urban rumours!' Bee is furious that Waverley is finally getting feedback.

'No, I'm interested to hear what he has to say, Beatrice.'

There's a collective intake of breath. No one uses Bee's real name. Ever. She and Victor obviously have some kind of history. But how come?

Jay is already trotting out the old scare story about evil drug dealers dishing out drugged kiddie tattoos outside the local junior school.

Leo laughs. 'That's not outrageous, just stupid. There's no profit in handing out free drugs to little kids.'

'And he would know,' Marlon whispers.

A girl puts her hand up. 'That story about the man who flushed the baby alligators down the toilet, is that an urban legend?'

Waverley smiles. 'Tell us the story and we'll decide.'

We have to listen to the tired old yarn about the baby alligators that grew too big for their tanks. The owner flushed them down the toilet. Instead of drowning, the reptiles began mutating in the sewers. Durn *durn* DURN . . .

Victor is making a list on the board. Toxic tattoos, sewer alligators.

Jay splutters, 'Imagine what a big daddy alligator would do to you when it came back UP the toilet to get its revenge!'

Slowly but surely the class is coming out of its Friday afternoon coma. Waverley knows exactly which buttons to press and I don't like it. Judging from the look on her face, nor does Bee.

In a twinkling, we've moved on to serial-killer legends. The psycho on the internet who styles himself the Slave Master. The Cinema Killer, whose fave form of homicide is booting girls over cinema balconies, and the pervert with a hook for a hand, who prefers to off young couples while they're doing the deed in daddy's car.

Kids my age will happily talk about serial killers all day. Waverley's got them all eating out of his hand. He's playing with us. It's almost like he wants to make something happen.

Outside, the storm is hurling itself at the windows, making the glass rattle in the frames. Inside, Waverley is still compiling his list. 'This is all excellent stuff. You're on the right track,' he enthuses, 'but these are universal legends. I'd like to hear stories peculiar to this area. Anyone know any local urban legends?'

The room actually seems to change shape, like a room in a dream.

There are things you just don't say to adults. There are things you don't even totally believe yourself. But when you're alone in the dark, they come back to haunt you just the same.

The class is stunned into silence. Then Roshelle loses it. 'You don't mean those stories about Mortagaine House?' she babbles.

Someone gasps, and everyone starts talking at once.

Waverley's voice cuts through the mayhem. 'One at a time!' He gives Roshelle an encouraging smile. 'You first.'

She's so nervous, she can't stop grinning. 'OK, well, erm, Mortagaine House is a really old building, and it's quite tall, fourteen floors. But when they numbered the flats, the council, or whoever, said they couldn't have a thirteenth floor. It might be bad luck. So on the landings and the lift panel, the numbers like, jump from twelve to fourteen. But my friend's cousin used to clean windows for the council and he told her that if you count from the outside of the building, you know, in a certain light? You can definitely see an extra floor between floors twelve and fourteen.'

Roshelle has been fighting a losing battle with hysterics. Now she collapses into helpless giggles.

Jude immediately jumps in. 'I know this kid who saw the thirteenth floor through the lift gates. He said there was this like, icy void.'

Leo shakes his head. 'Nah, man, it's hot. Hot and stinky like the snake house. That's what I heard!'

'They could both be true,' suggests Tariq. 'Maybe everyone has a unique experience.'

Marlon shakes his head. 'No, there's that thing, remember? The listener or whatever they call it.'

A collective shudder goes through the class.

Waverley looks blank. 'The *listener*?'

'You never see it,' Leo explains. 'You just feel it listening to your thoughts. People say it taps into your mind.' He swallows. 'Sometimes it talks.'

Against my will, the back of my neck starts to creep.

Natz's hand shoots up. 'My best friend's brother went up in the goods lift,' she says in an awed voice. 'He was helping a mate move house. The lift jammed between floors and he was stuck there with this massive chest of drawers and this disembodied voice started talking to him.'

Everyone gasps.

'Darren said it was like the voice *knew* all this deeply personal stuff about his life. Stuff no one could possibly know.'

Shut up, I want to tell them. Just shut UP. But now they've started, they can't stop, or they just don't know where to stop. In no time they're mixing local legends with dross from Sunday tabloids, or satellite TV.

Elvis Presley didn't really snuff it. The king of rock'n' roll is still strumming 'Blue Suede Shoes' up on the thirteenth floor. And contrary to rumour, wolves didn't die out. Oh, no. On clear moonlit nights you can hear them howling down the lift shaft of Mortagaine House.

And don't forget the evil scientists plotting to create a genetically modified race and take over the world . . .

'Let me get this straight,' Waverley says. 'You're suggesting this mansion block has a supernatural floor which functions as a portal into another kind of reality? One with totally different rules?'

'Yes, yes!' everyone says excitedly. They've trusted

an adult with their bizarre secret and he doesn't think they're crazy!

Waverley frowns. 'But there's no evidence, surely?'

Leo flushes as if he's been slapped. 'These things happened, man.'

Jude backs him up. 'For real!'

There's an uncomfortable silence. No one looks at anyone else.

Natz says, 'There was that kid who disappeared at Halloween.'

Roshelle gasps. 'I'd forgotten him!'

'There was more than one,' Jude says darkly.

'No end of kids disappeared over the years,' agrees Leo. 'They just hush it up.'

'Let's stick with the first boy,' says Waverley. 'Do we have a name?'

'Martin Coombs!' Natz answers so fast, you can tell she thinks about this story a lot. She looks uncertainly around the class. 'It was about twenty years ago, wasn't it? Yeah, twenty years. Martin and his mates had all heard the rumours about Mortagaine House. Martin was a bit of a daredevil and he decided they should check it out for themselves.'

Jay quickly hijacks her story. 'But his mates wimped

28

out, so Martin said he'd go on his own. He went up in that lift at midnight on Halloween and never came down. He's never been seen again.'

Waverley's done something I'd have thought was impossible: taken a rabble of jaded Friday afternoon teenagers and turned them into one completely freaked near-hysterical unit.

Everyone except Bee Molloy and me.

'The boy actually disappeared from the area?' Mr Waverley inquires in a neutral, therapist's tone.

'Totally,' says Jay. 'Ask anyone.'

'Kids vanish every day, you muppet,' I jeer. 'There's nothing supernatural about it. They fall off motorway bridges, crash stolen cars into walls, hitch rides with pervy strangers, fall under trains. Kids are an endangered species. It's a fact of life –'

The bell goes in the middle of my big speech. Usually there's a mad Friday afternoon stampede. But my classmates seem unnaturally subdued, collecting up bags and books, avoiding each other's eyes. They look ridiculously young suddenly. Waverley has exposed the needy little kids beneath our sneery teen defences. I really hate him for that.

I storm up to him, pushing my face into his. 'What

were you playing at just then?'

Waverley looks mildly surprised. 'I thought you might learn something about your locality. Didn't you?'

'You can't teach me anything, man! I live in those flats, and there is no magic land at the top of the Faraway Tree. Sorry to disappoint you.'

Bee is carefully looping her scarf around her neck, giving no sign she's paying attention to this conversation, yet I feel she's listening to every word.

'I'm not disappointed!' Waverley says cheerfully. 'If I've got a healthy debate going, I know I'm doing something right! Incidentally, I'm setting you an assignment,' he says over his shoulder, as he scrubs all traces of his handwriting off the board. 'I want you to go to the local library tomorrow. Research Mortagaine House scare stories. Find some solid basis for refuting them, since you despise them so much. Beatrice here can help you.'

I'm speechless. This guy is telling us to go to the library! In our own *time*! What century does he think this is? Bee and I refused to play his little teacher's game, so now he's got to get us back.

I don't even look at Bee. I don't have to. Our connection is suddenly so strong, I can practically feel thought-impulses flashing between us like Morse code.

'No problem,' I tell Waverley. 'You want evidence, we'll get evidence. Isn't that right?' I say to Bee.

'Sure. You're on.'

She's cucumber cool, but I know she's as bewildered as I am.

'We'll hit the library tomorrow then,' I say. '2 p.m. suit you?'

Bee's friends sweep her off in a tide of giggles.

Marlon bangs me on the back. 'Good to see you've been taking lessons from the don. That was smooth. That was nice, man!'

'Woo!' says Jude. 'Bee Molloy's going to help Dino with his *research*!'

We join the crowd of kids streaming out of school.

I pull up my hood, put my head down and since I don't have a choice, I start the long grim walk back to Mortagaine House.

Bee and her friends wait, gossiping, on the crowded platform. The other girls squabble cheerfully about where to meet up later that night. Bee seems to be in another world, as her thumb expertly flicks the tiny buttons on her phone. Her face is supermodel cool, but

31

inwardly she's in uproar. It totally threw her, bumping into Dino in the corridor like that. When he deliberately took her side against Victor, she felt even more confused. Surely her former childhood sweetheart hadn't really received her silent SOS?

She swallows and reads the broken sentences on the tiny screen.

> *Dino, im scared im going crazy*
> *its one thing 2 believe in magic*
> *when yr a kid, but when yr own dad . . .*

'Ooh,' says Persia, scenting scandal. 'Who're you texting, girl?'

Bee hastily presses C for cancel. 'No one.'

The train roars in and she follows her friends into a carriage.

Stupid, stupid, she's so stupid. If she and Dino had a genuine connection, he'd have known why, today of all days, she had to show Victor where he stood, why she had to make him understand he couldn't just waltz in and take her father's place. But Dino didn't have a clue, he was just out for trouble like a typical boy.

Plus if they were true soulmates, she wouldn't need to text him; he'd see through the cool, glossy exterior to the churning mess underneath.

If he had any idea what was going on in Bee's home life, he couldn't let her walk away feeling so alone.

CHAPTER 2

THE batteries in my Walkman are dead. I'm having to walk along this squalid road without tunes. Without my favourite sounds for insulation, I'm a human sponge, soaking up each and every depressing sight along with the fumes.

'It's going to be great,' Dad said last night as he parked the rental van. 'You'll be in the thick of things. You'll be where the action is.'

Where the dross is, more like.

I pass at least five homeless people. One is just a girl, with raw chapped-looking hands and scary vacant eyes. I see these people but I don't look at them. I put my head down and keep walking.

A drunk stumbles alongside me, yelling, 'The price is too high. The price is too high!'

'Yeah, whatever, Grandad,' I say.

Dad's always telling me, 'It doesn't cost anything to be nice, Dino.'

Well, that's pure lies. Being nice cost Dad his house, his business, even his health. There's no way he'd be on blood pressure pills if it wasn't for the bankruptcy. Now the bank won't let him have his own cheque book. Mum has to do it all. How humiliating is that?

My dad's the best but people see him coming. I'm not like that. I've got three rules I stick to, no matter what.

1. *Look out for you and yours, because no one else will.*
2. *Never tell outsiders your private business.*
3. *Don't give your power away. People take advantage.*

That's why I refused to join in that sensation-fest in Waverley's class just now. Voices in lifts, dark forces capable of luring innocent kids in off the street. That stuff could prey on your mind. Then where'd you be? Out on the street probably, raving on to yourself like that old alkie.

A fleet of emergency vehicles comes whooping and wailing down the street. Cars and buses frantically change lanes. I watch the chilling blue flicker go zigzagging through the dark, and I think, my family doesn't deserve this.

Someone has gone from one end of the street to the other, putting up pitiful home-made posters. 'Have you seen this boy? Carl Rivers aged fourteen years. Last seen 15 September.'

The heavy rain has already washed away all the personal characteristics that made Carl Carl. The blurred features could belong to any missing white youth. He could be me.

I hurry past a tanning parlour, a pizza place, the local fire station, cut down an alley, and then my heart drops into my trainers.

There it is – home sweet home – stretching three-quarters of the way down Paris Gardens, and bending around into Monkwell Place. With its rows of tiny windows, Mortagaine House looks more like one of Her Majesty's prisons than a mansion block.

A homeless kid huddles outside our entrance. An ancient knitted hood is pulled down over his face to keep out the rain. He isn't begging, just sitting on his tatty cardboard with a skinny dog curled up beside him. I jog past them into the lobby and the roar of wind, rain and traffic cuts out, as if I've been plunged underwater.

Inside, it's like some tired old museum. Faded wall tiles with faded writing. Ancient Greek-style pillars with paint peeling off.

Even the air feels tired as if our oxygen quota is somehow being used up before it reaches us.

I wait for the lift and I don't hear one sign of life. No footsteps, no radios, no clunk of taps turning off and on, no flushing toilets, not even a good old-fashioned family row. Just the creak-creak-creak of the antiquated lift in the shaft. Sometimes I wonder if anyone else actually lives here.

The cage lowers itself into view. I drag back the heavy iron gates with their old-fashioned twiddles and twirls, hop in, close them and press fourteen, the top button on the panel. It lights up like a round yellow eye.

There's a pause, then the lift lurches upward. It creaks ponderously from landing to landing. *Ten, eleven, twelve.* There's a sickening jolt.

Fourteen. There you go, I tell myself. What was so hard about that?

I let myself in the flat and squeeze down the hallway between the unpacked boxes. The air smells of cleaning fluid. My parents are in the sitting room, washing down walls. Dad's up the stepladder, doing parts Mum can't reach.

'I see this more as an opportunity,' Mum is telling my dad. 'Now we get to rethink our priorities. It's a new beginning.'

'And these views!' says Dad. 'People would kill for views like these.'

It's the new family game. Reasons to be happy your father went bankrupt. Mum sees me in the doorway and looks horrified. 'Is it that time already?'

'Gee thanks, how was your day, Mum?'

She ruffles my hair with a wet hand. 'You know I didn't mean it like that, petal.'

'How's it looking?' Dad calls. 'I think it's looking better.'

Homesickness is a lot like seasickness. Both make you lose all will to live. The difference is, seasickness ends when you reach your destination. This IS my destination.

I never gave our old house much thought while we were living there. It was just our house. It felt right. It even smelled right.

All day, my parents have been ripping up disgusting old carpet, scrubbing down walls. But this morgue will never be home.

I wander into the kitchen and peer in the fridge. My heart sinks. Mum and Dad have been too busy to make it to the supermarket. I'm just wondering if it would be tactless to ask your bankrupt parents to order in from the local pizzeria when the phone rings.

'It's Auntie Tippie,' I report back. 'She's been cooking all day and wants to know when it's OK to bring it round.'

Mum wilts against my dad. 'I don't think I've got the energy for your sister.'

Aunt Xanthippe has a big heart but her visits tend to involve the kind of security precautions reserved for American presidents. First Dad has to phone for a taxi to collect her. A black cab, not a minicab. All minicab drivers are murderers, according to my aunt. Then I have to zoom downstairs, ready to dash out the instant the taxi appears. If my aunt doesn't see a familiar face, she can't even get out of the car. I hang around the silent lobby, keeping a wary eye on the street.

A young woman – just a girl really – struggles in out of the rain. Her teeny-weeny see-through umbrella has turned inside out. She's soaked to the skin and hugely pregnant, yet she's laughing, as if she thinks it's a riot. 'Hi! What a day!' she says breathlessly.

The girl drips her way over to the lift, dumps her bags, and begins to haul energetically at the gates. I'm worried she'll do herself some damage so I rush to help.

'You angel,' she says gratefully. As she sails up out of sight, she calls, 'Byee, Sir Galahad!'

I'm smiling to myself. She's got to be a nut-case, but she's definitely the happiest person I've seen in a long while. My cousin Helen was just the same when she was having Katinka.

A car hoots and I charge out into the street. A middle-aged woman in dark glasses peers anxiously out from the back of a cab. She sees me and lets out the breath she's been holding. I relieve her of the Tupperware and help her out. As usual Aunt Xanthippe is made up to the nines. Like her sunglasses, this is for defence purposes only. The more layers Aunt Tippie has between herself and the scary outside world, the safer she feels. She hooks a trembling arm through mine. 'Dino, you darling boy!' she says brightly. 'You get better-looking every time I see you!'

Like a horse-whisperer soothing a panicky pony, I coax her away from the cab, across the pavement and into the lift. Aunt Tippie is not only scared of open spaces and minicabs. She's also scared of small enclosed spaces. If you look at it like that, simply bringing us a meal from the other side of town is a major heroic feat.

Mum and Dad show her round the new flat, and she admires everything several times, even forcing herself to look out of the window, so she can marvel queasily at the cityscape below. 'This place is going to be a palace by the time you've finished,' she insists.

'By the time Diane's finished,' Dad corrects her. 'I'm just the hired hand!'

Mum swats him. 'Don't make out you're a hen-pecked husband, Kostos Skerakis. Your sister knows that isn't true!'

Our real crockery is still in boxes, so we have to eat Aunt Tippie's food off plastic picnic plates. Mum keeps apologising. Each time, my aunt says, 'It's *you* I've come to see, Diane, not your china!'

Aunt Tippie doesn't get out much, for obvious reasons, so when she does she goes manic. She talks non-stop through the meal, hardly drawing breath. My cousin Helen's husband has finally found a job after years of hanging around the Jobcentre, which goes to show that where there's life there's hope. The fairy dress Mum and Dad bought Katinka for her birthday is a huge success.

'Helen keeps asking, "How come Kostos and Diane picked such a perfect present!"' My aunt beams around the table.

She's trying to make us feel better, reassuring my parents that the downturn in our fortunes is a temporary glitch, but their smiles get increasingly strained.

By Greek standards we're a small family. But it must be half an hour at least before Dad's sister runs out of news. Personally I'm OK with silence, but to Aunt Xanthippe it's like wind whistling across the prairies. She starts to babble wildly about a travel book she's reading.

'You should go there, Xanthippe,' Mum says in a tired voice. 'Wouldn't you like to go to Arizona and see those fabulous canyons for yourself, instead of just reading about them?'

My aunt's eyes grow huge. 'I couldn't! Who'd look after the cats?'

Dad gives her back a soothing rub. 'Tippie's a home bird. She likes her home comforts.'

Aunt Tippie eventually exhausts herself, not to mention everyone else, and Dad and I put her back in a taxi. Fifteen minutes later on the dot, she rings to let us know she's safely home.

She never used to be this timid. I remember my tiny wild-haired aunt charging out of her house when two huge rough boys were fighting in the street, yelling, 'Would it kill you kids to play NICE?'

'One day your sister will run out of phobias,' Mum sighs. 'Then the world will end!'

My father shakes his head. 'Poor Tippie. So many dangers. Every night when she goes to bed, she thinks, A miracle, I survived!'

Mum plants a kiss on his bald spot. 'You see the best in people. That's why I married you.'

'Not true,' Dad says in a stage whisper. 'She married me because I was the best-looking hunk in town.'

'Go on believing that, old man, if it helps!' I tease.

I watch TV with them, until it's time to hook up with Marlon and the others. There's nothing on TV worth watching. I'm just being friendly.

We're doing our best, Mum, Dad and me. But it's like we're killing time till we can go back home. Unfortunately, as of yesterday 'home' officially ceased to exist. Now it's purely a mark on a map.

'What's done is done,' I heard my mum tell Dad on our last night in the old house. 'From now on, we just look forward.'

The thing is I'm not sure any of us knows how. Meanwhile we all pretend to be riveted by the sight of a beaming construction worker emerging from a cloud of dry ice.

'I think he's very convincing,' Mum says.

'He *looks* like a celebrity,' Dad agrees. 'He's got something.'

'You certainly don't get many brickies that confident in gold lurex,' I say with a straight face.

We watch a few more wannabes impersonating famous singers none of us has ever heard of, then I go to get changed.

Most of my stuff is still in boxes and it takes a while to locate some suitable clothes. I throw on the last cool gear I'll ever be able to afford, splash on the sexy cologne and I'm ready for action.

As I leave, Dad is hunting through boxes in the kitchen. 'Where did she put those painkillers?' he mutters. He sees me in the doorway and waggles his bushy eyebrows. 'Which lucky girl are you dancing with tonight, Konstandino?'

'For the umpteenth time, we don't have to dance *with* anyone, Dad,' I tell him. 'We're not obsessed with that cheesy girl-boy scenario like your lot. We can have sex any time we want. We go clubbing for the vibes and the music.'

He pretends to stagger with horror. 'What did I tell you?' he calls to Mum. 'Our son's a mutant!'

I'm already out of the door, laughing.

When I finally float back up in the lift in the early hours, I'm in a fuzzy pink cloud. Every muscle feels happily pliable like warm plasticine. Bankruptcy courts, power-mad supply teachers, supernatural voices, can't touch me. It isn't drink, drugs or sex. I've danced myself into a state of pure bliss. My world is beautiful and, for a change, absolutely nothing hurts.

I've been waiting outside the library for ten minutes.

I started out leaning against a wall, hands in pockets, my streetwise hero pose. But the east wind is vicious, so now I'm pacing and shivering, which doesn't look so cool. Times like this, I'm tempted to take up smoking. It might kill you but it *oozes* style.

It seemed natural yesterday, fixing up to research urban legends with the school princess. But today it seems like a very bad idea. I'm going to humiliate myself big time, and I'd like to get it over with asap.

Bee Molloy appears at the bottom of the steps, bang

45

on quarter past, wearing a black puffa jacket and jeans, and chatting animatedly into her phone. As she talks, she keeps pushing her glossy curls out of her eyes, and once again I have that niggling sense that something's different. Isn't she much paler than usual? No, it's the hair, it's shorter, that's it.

'Yeah later,' Bee says into her phone.

'Hi,' she says to me and shoots me a coded smile. *Don't think you can try anything,* and I shoot a coded smile right back. *As if!*

Bee isn't what you'd call tall, five foot three max, but she's the coolest girl I know. It isn't her clothes, or even her looks. It's something that shines out of her, even when she's in a foul mood, like now.

'OK, what's the strategy?' she sighs.

'I thought we'd dig out background info on Mortagaine House. Then look for specifics on that kid who disappeared. Does that sound OK?'

'I suppose.' Bee seems unconvinced.

'What would you do?' I ask.

'I wouldn't be here, obviously?' she flashes. 'It wasn't *my* idea, if you remember.'

I knew this was a big mistake. I let my hormones get the upper hand, deluding myself that Bee felt the twang of our old connection, when she just wanted to annoy Victor Waverley for mysterious reasons of her own.

'Erm, hello?' I say in my coldest voice. 'It's my weekend too, you know. So, since neither of us wants to be here, let's just get on with it and then we can go.'

We do a lightning swoop on the local history section. Bee flicks through her pile, visibly cheesed off.

'Waverley really seems to get under your skin,' I say after a while.

She scowls. 'You have NO idea.'

'How d'you know each other, if you don't mind me asking?'

Bee looks away. 'I'd rather not talk about it.'

'Sure, no problem.'

'If you must know, Victor and my mother are, erm . . .'

I gawp at her. 'Oh, *right*! Hard on you, if you don't like the guy.'

'That's the understatement of the year!' she snorts. 'I mean, you knew my dad? You remember what an amazing person he is?'

I remember a guy with disturbingly bright blue eyes, but I just nod to show sympathy.

'Victor just does youth work!' she says with contempt.

'You mean, he runs an actual youth club?'

'Some sad set-up for misfits. I didn't beg for details.' Her face twists. 'How *can* she?'

'Perhaps they have stuff in common?' I suggest.

'I refuse to think about what Victor and my mother have in common!' She glares at me. 'What's funny?'

'Don't know about you,' I say hastily, 'but I haven't found even one measly reference to Mortagaine House.'

She pushes a book across the table. 'I turned up a couple of pics.'

The first photo was taken at the end of the Second World War. Happy soldiers and civilians dancing a chaotic conga down Paris Gardens. Mortagaine House is only just visible through the fluttering Union Jacks.

The second is a much earlier street scene, dated June 1861, the year of some big world fair, and shows a Victorian traffic jam.

Omnibuses, horse-drawn cabs and carts choke the street. Stressed-looking city folk are grimly enduring the mayhem. It tickles me how they're all wearing hats. Even the urchin sweeping the crossing is peering out from under a grossly outsize cap. Looming over these dead-and-gone Victorians is Mortagaine House.

'It looks just the same.' I say gloomily. 'Exactly the same.'

'What did you expect? Ectoplasm oozing from the windows?'

Bee's attitude is really grating on my nerves.

'I didn't expect anything,' I snap. 'It'd just be convenient if we could find something to explain how these stories got started. Then we'd be in a stronger position at least.'

'Ooh, Dino!! Sounds like Victor got under your skin too!'

I take a deep breath. 'I suggest we scour the local newspapers.'

'Yay,' Bee says in a scornful voice. 'Dino Skerakis, ace reporter, is on the case. I can't believe you're so into this!'

I count very very slowly to ten. 'We started, that's all,' I say, 'so now we may as well finish.'

According to Natz, Martin vanished almost exactly twenty years ago, so we take over one of the library computers and flash up every edition of the evening paper for October that year.

And suddenly here it is. The unexplained disappearance of a ten-year-old boy called Martin Coombs on 31 October. He really did disappear on Halloween.

'That doesn't mean anything,' we say simultaneously.

I tell myself the date is a red herring. Hundreds of kids must have disappeared at Halloween over the years. Child murderers can strike at any time.

Missing kids are always big news for a few weeks, and the local police mounted a major operation. They searched abandoned buildings, combed waste ground, dragged rivers and canals, and the paper published the usual appeals for people to come forward.

We plough through cheesy quotes from neighbours and teachers, saying what a happy, sociable kid Martin was, and how he had no reason to run away from home.

'Like he'd tell them,' Bee mutters.

'You notice they never say what a miserable little git you were! Get bumped off, and all at once you're getting rave reviews!'

She doesn't smile. It's the news photos. We're both finding them more upsetting than we want to admit. Martin is a completely average ten-year-old kid. Fair hair, friendly grin. Yet his expression gives me the creeps. I've seen it before in pictures of kids who go missing, then turn up dead, or never turn up at all; and Martin's got that identical look. As if he knows something dark is going to happen and wishes someone could make it stop.

In the last photo, he's performing some fancy manoeuvre with his yo-yo, a dayglo orange number he'd had for years. Martin was crazy about that yo-yo, everyone said, took it everywhere, even slept with it under his pillow.

The story of the search for the missing boy ran through Christmas and into the new year. Then the paper got wind of some local sex scandal and Martin Coombs dropped out of sight. At no point did witnesses mention Mortagaine House. If you believed the papers, Martin had simply vanished off the face of the earth.

'So where does that leave us?' I say, half to myself.

Bee scowls. 'I knew it was a total waste of time.'

A woman behind us is making irritated huffing noises, clearly wanting us to get off the computer.

'No need to get yourself all bent out of shape,' I tell her. 'My parents pay taxes too.'

We drift back to our table.

I say, 'Erm, so what's your dad up to these days?'

There's a flicker of something in her eyes. 'Oh, you know Dad! Always got some scheme on the go. He's a neighbour of yours actually. He's still in our old flat.'

'I thought you guys used to live in St Clements?'

'We did, until my parents broke up. Before that they

had a flat in Mortagaine House. Dad kept it on for business reasons or something. When he and Mum split, he moved back in.' Her face clouds over. 'He lives there with his child bride now.'

'Sound as if you don't like her.'

Bee shrugs. 'Sadie's OK. Apart from the nightmare dress sense. Still that won't matter now she's –'

I'd swear she was going to tell me something, but she suddenly jumps up, scraping back her chair, talking so fast the words tumble over each other.

'I've got to go. It's Roshelle's birthday on Monday. I promised to help her find an outfit.'

I'm appalled. I can't believe Bee's running out on me to go shopping.

'But we haven't even got started! We're supposed to get evidence. You saw how Waverley was. He was totally patronising us. I'm not letting him get away with it.'

'Then get someone else to join your little crusade. I've got better things to do,' she snaps.

'But – but then –' I stammer.

'But what?' she says sharply.

'We'll look stupid,' I say in a feeble voice. 'And he'll think he's won.'

'He'll only win if we give up our entire Saturday to chase this stupid red herring. I'm out of here, OK?'

I can't explain, even to myself, why this feels so wrong.

Bee has a special technique for making her scarf hang exactly right. While she's perfecting her look, I slip a library book into my pocket, on the off-chance it contains vital info that just might salvage my reputation.

We walk out together into a cutting east wind.

'Later.' Bee shivers and hurries away.

'So you don't believe it either?' I call after her.

Bee turns. She's got her mobile in her hand, thumb at the ready. I wonder who she needs to text so urgently, she has to do it on the move.

'What don't I believe?' she says in a bored voice.

'That Mortagaine House is our local portal into hell?'

It's like I've slapped her. Her eyes go wide with shock. Then she gives a peal of scornful laughter, 'Dino, please! I enjoy Buffy as much as the next girl. But I don't want to *be* her, OK?'

She walks away so fast, she's practically running.

But I'm rooted to the spot. I'm having a flashback so vivid it takes my breath away. A pre-school Bee Molloy is disappearing out of the taverna, slumped over her daddy's shoulder like a sleepy little sack of potatoes. Passing headlights illuminate her face and I see a startling glint of gold.

Bee used to have a natural gold streak. Now it's gone. I can understand totally why she dyed it. Hair that freaky could make you feel things were expected of you, as if the god of DNA has marked you out for heroic deeds. Bee's a twenty-first-century girl. She likes to blend in and keep it light.

But as I watch her vanish in the crowd, all the colours drain from my world. I'm having one of my 'is this all there is?' moments, when everything I see is pointless or plain ugly, when I know, without a shadow of a doubt, that we're all alone in this world.

A woman with a toddler in a buggy is screaming at her boyfriend. 'You never see me. You don't see who I really am!'

'Well, you bloody suffocate ME!' he yells in her face. 'You don't see I've got to have my SPACE!' The words come out of a chat show. But their real-life misery curdles the air. The boyfriend storms off, jaw muscles clenched. Their baby stares after him with a bewildered expression.

I'll tell you how I feel. I feel like, long ago, we were

promised something better. But I'm the only idiot still waiting for it to show.

> *I cd have talked 2 the old magic dino*
> *where did u go? where did those 2 little magic*
> *kids go?*
> *its like we got lost in some dark woods & now we*
> *cant find our –*

Bee Molloy stares at her phone in dismay. What is she *doing*? Walking through a crowd of strangers, composing insane text messages to a boy who no longer exists?

She hits the cancel button and her message obediently disappears, leaving no sign it was ever there. So why does she feel a creeping chill, as if someone has been reading every word?

CHAPTER 3

IT'S two in the morning and there's some kind of party going on in a local warehouse. Far enough away that I can only hear the bass line, but close enough for the strangely trippy rhythms to make it impossible to sleep. The killer draught sneaking through the window frame is not helping. If I knew where my CDs were, I could listen to my disc player under my covers until I dozed off. That's if I knew where my disc player was.

Before the move, Mum had me running backwards and forwards to the local shops for boxes to pack our belongings. A good half of them are now lined up alongside my bed. It's like camping out in Cardboard City.

I try to make my mind clean and empty like in the yoga video Mum got Dad for his hypertension, but unwanted memories blow in like tumbleweed.

Like the legend of the lost children. They're not exactly lost, the poor kids never got any further than

Mortagaine House, but they can't go home, not now, not with the barcodes on their foreheads and their empty yellow eyes . . .

I snap on the bedside lamp and pad across to my clothes, extract the stolen library book from the heap and take it back to bed. I'll have to bore myself to sleep.

Propping myself on my elbow, I flick through the pages. Flick, flick. More old photos, mostly taken in Victorian times. Printed under each photograph is the month and year in which it was taken. I flip past long-gone hardware stores and chemists' shops, and rows of solemn boys and girls in knickerbockers and pinafores. Flick, flick. A works outing. Flick. A street scene of Paris Gardens taken in May 1861. Yawn. Flick.

I flick back. That can't be right. Where Mortagaine House ought to be, there's a public park with iron railings and a fancy gateway. A sign says TO THE GARDENS.

The Victorian traffic-jam picture was taken in June the same year. That's crazy! How could Mortagaine House have existed in June, but not in May? They printed the wrong date, I tell myself. Something that massive couldn't spring up overnight without people noticing.

Another unwanted memory blows into my mind.

I'm in a boarded-up house with other awe-struck kids.

In school, we can't listen to a teacher for two consecutive minutes, yet here we crouch on a dirty floor, soaking up Tina's words as if our lives depend upon it. I can still hear her voice, I can hear her exact words, as she tells the story of the true origins of Mortagaine House.

'One night, it sprouted up out of the ground in a massive ball of blue fire. The only people who saw it happen were the kind who didn't count. Tramps and madmen, kids who couldn't sleep. But when all the regular people woke up next morning and saw Mortagaine House stretching down Paris Gardens and into Monkwell Place, they didn't blink. They told each other that they actually *remembered* seeing it built.'

'It's like they were hypnotised,' says someone in a scared voice.

Tina rolls her eyes. 'ALL grown-ups are hypnotised, birdbrain. Except for one. Remember who that is?'

'The Guardian,' we chant obediently.

Not only did Tina Tillotson always tell the legends using exactly the same words, she always told them in strict rotation, like a tribal storyteller reciting ancestral tales. A good third of the legends concerned a character who was simply referred to as the Guardian: a charismatic Light Teacher supposedly hiding out underneath the city, waiting for the day when he would lead his secret army into battle against the evil presence on the thirteenth floor.

It sounds pathetic now, but I genuinely believed Tina was telling those stories just for me. Reminding me personally to be on the lookout, so I'd recognise this saviour when he eventually showed up. The Guardian legends made me feel as if I was living in a story too, a story where good triumphs and life finally makes sense.

I shut the book with a snap.

Life doesn't make sense. I found that out years ago. Last time I saw Tina Tillotson, she was sweeping up old mens' hair at the local barber's. There is no mysterious guardian who's going to come zooming to our rescue. We're all alone, on a spinning lump of rock. Nothing we do or say will change that. But most people can't live with this, so they make up elaborate explanations about good and evil, to explain why life basically sucks. And like Tina's legends, they're pure lies. OK, so you could say our city has more than its share of hard-luck stories. It doesn't *mean* anything.

Another ghostly tumbleweed bowls past. It's not

lost kids, I'm remembering this time, it's the story of Mimi Rousseau . . .

Not many people know this, but before *Souls for Sale* came out, the album that made her famous, Mimi rented a tiny bedsit at Mortagaine House. This was back in the days when she was singing in underground clubs, and waitressing at a place called the Sweet World Café to pay the bills. This was a bad time for Mimi. No one wanted to buy her weird little songs. Even her best friends were telling her she should get a real job.

This particular night, the night her luck finally changed, Mimi was going down with flu. But instead of going home, when she finished her waitressing shift she went into the staff loos and changed into a skimpy lace dress.

OK, I may have borrowed this detail from the mini-series, but for me the white lace dress, with its asymmetric hem, is a crucial part of Mimi's story, like her tousled red bed-hair. Like the hair, that dress said sexy but vulnerable. The moment she put it on, you knew she was going to get hurt, big time. Which is exactly what happened.

Mimi had promised to meet her boyfriend at a party. But when she walked in, the scumbag was flirting outrageously with another girl and Mimi rushed straight out in tears.

Next day she failed to turn up to work. This was completely unlike her. Her mates at Sweet World got so worried they went round to her bedsit and rang the bell. They could hear music playing but no one answered. They tried the door and it swung open. No Mimi. She'd just walked out, leaving the stereo on and the lights blazing. Hadn't even taken her coat.

Her friends rang around hospitals and called the police, but, like Martin, Mimi Rousseau had vanished without a trace.

Except Mimi came back.

Three days later her agent was woken by hammering on his door. It was Mimi, shivering in her skimpy dress, babbling about some wonderful song she'd composed. She insisted on playing it to him there and then.

You'll find the rest of the official bio inside any one of Mimi Rousseau's CDs. How she walked right past her agent, sat down at his piano and played the most beautiful song he'd heard in his entire professional career. The bio goes on to say that Mimi's success was all down to her incredible talent and persistence, blahdy blahdy blah.

The legend takes a different slant. The legend says when Mimi Rousseau left the party, she was so distraught she didn't care if she lived or died. Her love life was a disaster, like her non-existent singing career. Mimi fled back to her dingy pad, gulped down a bottle of cold cure, crawled into bed without undressing and cried herself to sleep.

An hour later, she was woken by a disembodied voice whispering in her ear. The voice knew all about Mimi, her dreams and failures, her two-timing love-rat boyfriend. It promised that if she did what she was told, her waitressing days would be over and she'd be a star, just like she always dreamed

I can picture the next part as vividly as if I'd seen it on *The Mimi Rousseau Story*. The door to Mimi's flat opens and she comes out, looking dazed in her crumpled lace. I even see the chipped silver nail varnish on her bare feet as she floats down the corridor and into the lift.

The light on the lift panel goes from ten to eleven, to twelve. Before it reaches floor fourteen, the lift stops without a sound.

The gates slide open as though they've been oiled, and Mimi steps out. I watch her bare feet disappear into swirls of mist.

Hours or it could be days later, she comes padding back. The hem of her dress is soaked and dark. Her feet look blue with cold. Mimi Rousseau doesn't feel a thing. All she can think about is the song burning inside her. The song that will bring her fame and fortune at last.

People say if you hold up the cover of *Souls for Sale* in front of the mirror, the name of the true songwriter will appear in letters of hellfire, one supernatural letter at a time. Others say if you can get hold of a rare vinyl copy of Mimi's album, and play it backwards, you'll hear the voice that spoke to her that night.

Ping! The bulb in my bedside lamp blows. I'm in pitch darkness for three seconds max, then I hit the central switch and I'm back in a room full of boxes, my heart pounding like a hammer.

Sleep is now obviously out of the question. I find my remote and flick through TV channels until I find an old horror movie. A hideous zombie is lumbering through the Haitian jungle in pursuit of a blonde in increasingly tattered clothing. Not much of a story, but

I'm a teenage male so any plot which requires a babe to expose ever more of her assets is basically OK with me. Somewhere between *The Zombies' Revenge* and whatever dross the channel shows next, I blank out.

The electric light and TV are still on when I open my eyes on Sunday morning. I'm awake but only technically. In my mind I'm still stumbling down the badly lit tunnels of my dreams. I was chasing something or I was being chased, but I never got to see what it was, I could just hear it breathing . . .

It slowly dawns on me that the persistent ring tone is not part of the Sunday soap. I dive for my mobile. 'Marly?'

'Nah, I'm no ghost, man,' Marlon says in his street voice. 'Plus I prefer to be known as the Don, innit? Ready to come an' flex, star?'

I feel as if I've been airlifted out of some dark place into pure sunshine. Just dreams, I think with relief. Everyone has bad dreams.

I snatch a clean T-shirt off the pile. 'With you in twenty. I'll grab a shower then I'll meet you at Daphne's, yeah?'

The original Daphne snuffed it years ago, but everyone still refers to the greasy spoon round the corner as Daphne's, and Louis, the chilled guy who runs the place, doesn't seem to mind.

Marlon and I generally hang out together on Sundays. On Mondays, my mate likes to talk up our weekend activities, saying we were cruising the neighbourhood to feel the heat of the streets and flexing on the front line. What we actually do is work our way through Daphne's humungous all-day breakfast, then wander down to the canal, to check out the street market.

They have all sorts down here: vintage clothes, designer rip-offs, knocked-off CDs and DVDs. In honour of Halloween, some local hippies have set up a craft stall decorated with pumpkin lanterns. A cute girl with a nose stud is arranging a display of chenille spiders. We stop to flirt.

'I thought Halloween was about the waning of the light,' Marlon says loudly. 'When did it get to be about fluffy spiders?'

The girl waves one in his face. 'Don't underestimate these babies! They're handmade by real witches.'

'And conveniently machine washable,' I say wittily.

Marlon flirts with the hippie girl for a while. I don't like to cramp his style, so I just watch the passing scene. I keep seeing beautiful girls in black puffa jackets and

65

experience a twinge of disappointment each time she turns out not to be Bee.

You can tell Marlon thinks he's getting somewhere with the hippie girl, then her boyfriend roars up on his motor bike. I'm worried my mate is going to get his nose punched in, so I quickly drag him off to the vinyl stall.

I'm nowhere near ready to DJ in public yet. But I'm constantly on the lookout for good tunes to mix. Next to friends and family, music is probably the single most important thing in my life. I don't mean the dross they put out on Radio 1. I'm talking about real music.

By the time we finish browsing, the sun is starting to set. It looks quite pretty with strings of fairy lights around the stalls and the streaks of colour reflecting back from the water. But once the sun goes down, the temperature plummets. We buy hot dogs in an attempt to warm ourselves up, then jog away from the waterfront.

'So how did your "research" go with Bee Molloy?' Marlon sniggers.

I shove him off the pavement. 'Sod off, you filthy-minded muppet.'

We can't go home, that'd be like admitting defeat, but we're desperate to get in out of the cold. Finally we sneak into one of the dodgier dockside pubs, on the off-chance they won't ask for ID. Marlon gets in a couple of pints without much hassle, and we spin them out for a good hour and a half. We even get to watch most of last night's footie on their widescreen TV, but then the landlord makes a big production of removing our empty glasses and we have to go back out into the night.

Almost immediately, we run into Jude and his mates. They're off to catch a retro horror show at the old Nero Picture House. We haven't got anything better to do, so we tag along. Judging from the queues, every teenager in the area had the same idea.

In an era of huge multiplexes, the Nero's owners decided to turn back the clock. The idea seems to be to recreate the original bona fide moviegoing experience for people who missed it first time around.

The decor certainly has that authentic tacky feel, tacky gold fixtures and fittings, dusty red velvet. The smell of fresh paint doesn't entirely hide the stink of damp. Maybe that's supposed to add to the ambience.

I peer around the audience, in case Bee is here with her mates, but at that moment the lights go down and the curtain swooshes back and I settle down in my punishingly hard seat to watch the film.

Even in a crowded cinema full of rustling and munching, *Nightmare on Elm Street* still gives me the chills. I can literally feel it peeling back all my defences and exposing the cowardly jelly inside.

When it's over we file back out into the cold. Everyone is visibly shaken.

'I hope Wes Craven dies and goes to hell!' Marlon is so churned up he actually forgets to do his gangster shtick.

'Why? It's a kicking film,' says one of Jude's mates.

'That creep robbed me of my childhood, man!' Marlon says. '*Elm Street* gave me night terrors for years.'

'Same here!' shudders one of the girls. 'I don't know why I keep putting myself through this.'

'For me it's a test,' says Marlon. 'I tell myself I'm bigger than that, you know? But freaking Freddie gets to me every time.'

'I couldn't sleep for months, the first time I saw it,' I admit.

'You're all a load of wusses,' Jude jeers.

'There's nothing wussy about us, man,' Marlon tells him. 'Freddie Kruger is the ultimate figure of terror – a disembodied child-killer who literally gets inside kids' dreams. Don't deny that idea scares you shitless, because that's pure lies!'

We walk along, arguing and asserting our teenage right to take up the whole pavement. At the fire station, we split and go our separate ways. After getting off to a weird start, it's been a surprisingly good day. Dad's right. I am in the thick of things down here. Mortagaine House could even turn out to be quite cool.

As I jog across Paris Gardens, I'm mentally reorganising my room to look less like a box depot, and more like the pad of a future international DJ. I swing in through the front door of Mortagaine House with my imaginary entourage and give myself a cheer, 'Yo! DJ Skerakis is in the house!' then freeze with embarrassment.

Waiting by the lift, shivering and wiping her eyes, is Bee Molloy.

CHAPTER 4

I'VE been thinking about her all day, but she didn't look like this. She must have rushed into the night in her old sweats and hoodie. There are panda smudges under her eyes where she's been crying.

When Bee sees me, her face crumples.

'I didn't know where else to go,' she sobs. 'I had to get out. I just couldn't stay in the house another minute!'

I'm still in shock at finding my childhood sweetheart in the lobby – plus I'm recovering from my humiliating entrance – but I know I'm supposed to say something, so I say gruffly, 'Want to tell me what happened?' which makes me sound like one of those old-style male movie stars.

'No!' she wails. 'It's too weird. I feel like I'm trapped in this – this *nightmare*.'

I'm useless when girls cry. And this isn't any girl, this is THE girl.

What am I going to do with her? If I take her up to

the flat, Dad will do his meaningful eyebrow-waggling and Mum'll get that lurve-light in her eye. Finally, her son brings a girlfriend home!

We can't stand here all night, so finally I take her to Daphne's, where I scrape up enough cash to buy us both a cup of tea. No disrespect to Louis, but his café is exceptionally depressing at this time of night: sad cabbies with body odour and sadder women wearing too much make-up. But on the upside, one more female in distress won't exactly attract attention.

I should try to find out what's wrong. But tact is not my strong point. Then there's the crying. If I pry into her private business, Bee might get even more upset. Right now, it's taking all her concentration just to control her cup.

I feel myself go hot and cold. I think I know why Bee was so upset when Victor Waverley turned up at our school. I know why Bee had to rush out into the night.

'Did Waverley hurt you?' I blurt out. 'Because –'

Before I embarrass myself any further, she gives a teary giggle. 'You've really got to stop watching Jerry Springer! This has nothing to do with Victor. He's so worried about corrupting me, he never even stays over.'

'Sorry. I didn't mean to – I just thought –'

71

Bee briefly closes her eyes. 'Look, I'm just going to tell it how it happened. But you're not going to believe it. I don't even believe it myself.'

'Don't worry about it,' I say. 'Just blurt it out.'

But my belly is churning. Something inside me seems to know that after this, nothing will ever be the same.

Bee takes a breath. 'A couple of nights ago my dad came round. It was late and Mum had gone to bed. She's a social worker – you knew that, right? And her caseload just wears her out. I let him in. He'd been drinking. Dad often drank when he and Mum were breaking up, but I'd never seen him like this.'

Her voice goes harsh with hurt. 'We used to be really tight, Dad and me. But last night, it was like I didn't know him.'

She forces herself to go on. 'Mum came down and packed me off to bed, but something felt off, so I listened on the stairs. Dad kept saying he'd done something terrible, but it had happened so long ago, he was a different person now, wah wah wah.'

'Do you think he had an affair?'

'I wish!' she says fervently. 'That would be, like, *normal*.' She takes a shaky breath. 'He went all around

72

the houses at first, but finally Dad told Mum what was worrying him. A few months ago Sadie got pregnant.'

'The girlfriend with no dress sense?'

'The worst. The point is my dad's not, like, one of the world's natural fathers, so he went into a total panic. But pretty soon Sadie got him happily brainwashed into the whole Daddy and Mummy Bear scenario.' Bee gives me a watery grin. 'That girl might dress like a flower fairy, but she has a mind like a steel trap.' Her eyes cloud. 'What was I saying?'

'Daddy and Mummy Bear.'

She scowls. 'Yuck, don't remind me. Stencilling the nursery, buying sweet ickle garments. Everything was just too lovely for words! And then Dad started having visions.'

I'm not sure I've heard her. 'Visions? What, like Joan of Arc?'

Bee sits back. I see this quiver go through her. 'Dino, let me give you a tiny tip. If someone tells you their father is having visions, it's probably better not to ask what kind. OK?'

I want to kick myself.

'Sorry,' I say awkwardly. 'No, I mean it. I'd be freaked too, if it was me.'

'Trust me, we haven't nearly reached the freaky part yet. My dad believes these hallucinations or whatever go back to something that happened while they were still living at Mortagaine House.'

It's suddenly hard to make my voice work. 'Oh, right.'

No wonder Bee wasn't keen to do Victor's research. It must have been way too close to home.

She's talking again. 'Dad says it happened just after they had me. Adopted me, I should say.' Bee shoots a glance from under her lashes. 'You did know about that?'

I didn't, but I shrug as if it's no big deal.

'Dad was having big financial problems around that time. He was terrified Mum would find out. My mother thinks if you owe money it's like the first step on the slippery slope to bankruptcy.'

She's not getting in a dig, I tell myself quickly. Bee probably hasn't even heard about my old man going bust.

'Anyway, like a total idiot, he borrowed from a local loan shark. But of course he couldn't pay it back so they turned nasty.'

'Like they do,' I sigh, still thinking of my dad.

'Dad said he was literally contemplating suicide. Then one night, he –' Bee takes a breath. 'My father said something came into the room and – and spoke to him.'

All the tiny hairs are standing up on the back of my neck, but I just say, 'OK.'

'The voice promised to solve all Dad's problems. All he had to do was go up to the thirteenth floor and do exactly what he was told.'

'Sheesh,' I mutter.

Bee's eyes flicker in my direction. 'Mum said he was dreaming, but Dad wouldn't have it. He started on about how the thirteenth floor really exists. He said he sees it every time he closes his eyes.'

'Your father *went* to the thirteenth floor?'

She scrubs her hand across her face, making new smudges.

'He says that's where he made the deal.'

It's suddenly impossible to breathe. I try not to picture Jimmie Molloy's hairy naked feet vanishing into the mist. *The Mimi Rousseau Story* has just morphed into something deeply chilling.

'He made a deal?' I croak. 'Who *with*?'

'Dad sidestepped that part. He just said he struck a bargain with an "unknown benefactor". It was agreed that my dad would win enough money on the horses to

75

pay off his debts et cetera, in return, erm, in return for – well, *me*.'

My jaw drops open. 'You're kidding!'

Bee shakes her head. 'No I'm not.'

'They'd just got this new little baby and your dad calmly agrees to hand you over! For *money*! That's disgusting!'

There's an electric silence. Bee jumps up, spilling tea. She's trembling. 'Do you think exposing my personal problems gives me some sick *thrill*?'

'Of course not – I just –'

'Well, whatever,' she says carelessly. 'It's not as if I seriously expected a basketball player to understand.'

'Bee, can you just –? I was shocked, OK? Can you just please tell me what happened.'

Bee sits down. She's still trembling, but she's back in control.

'There's not much more,' she says grimly. 'Everything goes according to plan. Dad's supernatural benefactor honours their bargain and Dad has his obscenely huge win. A few weeks later Mr Nobody wakes my dad in the night and tells him it's time to collect.' Bee gives an edgy laugh. 'Want to hear the punchline?'

I nod nervously.

'My old man says, "Yeah, well you can't have her because she's not my real flesh and blood, you sucker!"'

She's looking everywhere except at me. When Bee can finally meet my eyes, the hurt and bewilderment in her face makes me want to go and find Jimmie Molloy and punch his lights out. I have to fight to keep the contempt out of my voice.

'Confident bloke, your father, isn't he?' I say at last.

'Overconfident as it turns out. Now, if you believe Dad, it's payback time.'

'You do know this all sounds, you know, *mad*.'

Bee rubs at her eyes. She looks as if she wants to put her head down among the dirty cups and sleep for a year.

'You know the scary part?' she says shakily. 'I'm sure Dad thinks he's telling the truth. Maybe the thought of taking responsibility for a new baby is making him crack up. Or, equally depressing scenario, Dad's druggy youth just caught up with his brain cells.'

'It does sound like he's having some kind of breakdown.'

She gives me a tremulous smile. 'And then there's also this other outrageous possibility.'

I feel a flash of something. Not exactly fear. More like things are moving too fast for me to keep a grip.

'You mean he might be telling the truth?'

'I won't know, will I, until I've checked it out? So I'm going to see for myself. A kind of scientific experiment.'

I feel as if I'm in danger of spinning off into an alternative universe. 'You're seriously going to try to find the thirteenth floor?'

I almost say, *Are you seven?*

She darts a look at me. 'Erm – I was hoping you'd come with me.'

I'm weirdly flattered. 'Oh, right. Why me?'

'Because I don't want this getting all around the school, and you don't seem like the usual male blabbermouth.'

That's not quite so flattering.

'Sure,' I tell her. 'If you're completely –'

'When?' she interrupts fiercely.

'Whenever you like.'

'Tomorrow? After school?'

'Sure.' The coolest girl in the school has just handed me the opportunity to look like a hero. Since the thirteenth floor doesn't actually exist, how can I lose?

'Hang on,' I remember. 'We've got a match coming up. It'll have to be after basketball practice.'

Bee draws herself up to her full five foot three. 'You want me to wait around while you play some stupid *sport?*'

'You stood me up to buy a stupid dress,' I remind her.

> *do u ever feel like u r trapped in a bad movie?*
> *like, u want to be living yr life 4 real, but its 2 hard,*
> *& sometimes its not pretty, so u act this part and it*
> *gets harder & harder 2 stop.*
> *i thought maybe u feel that way too?*
> *that's y i came 2 find u 2night, but telling u about*
> *my dad felt like peeling off my skin, letting u see the*
> *real me made me feel ugly & exposed*
> *but u were so sweet,*
> *u didn't believe a word, yet u promised 2 help.*
> *its 1.30 in the morning & i must be in big trouble*
> *b/c it feels like u r the only real friend i have in this*
> *world – i*

Bee presses the delete key, watching nervously until every letter of her garbled email is wiped from her computer screen. She doesn't really believe her father's story, so why is she so scared about tomorrow? Why is she sitting in front of her computer in her fluffy white robe, forcing herself to stay awake, endlessly composing and deleting emails? And what will she do, if Dino turns out to be like everyone else in her life, and lets her down?

Next morning I catch Victor Waverley going into the staffroom and give him my half-page report.

He scans it in the doorway. 'So there was a real Martin Coombs.' His voice is so neutral, I can't tell if he's surprised.

'We couldn't find a single connection between Martin's disappearance and Mortagaine House,' I say. 'If you ask me, the Martin Coombs story just got added on with Elvis and the aliens, because –'

Waverley interrupts brusquely. 'Is this all you found out?'

'Pretty much, yeah. It still took up all bloody Saturday afternoon.'

I've decided not to tell Waverley about the picture in which Mortagaine House has mysteriously gone missing.

'Then you'd better read this.'

Waverley practically forces a book into my hands.

'Euch,' I say squeamishly, 'this the best copy you've got?'

It's not a book so much as a manky handful of pages. The cover is visibly rotting away. It smells of mildew and old cellars.

Marlon is whingeing behind me. 'I'm starving to death here, man. All the chips will be gone by the time we get there.'

'No thanks,' I tell Waverley. 'I wrote your pointless report. That's it.' I try to give it back but he won't take it.

'This book is by a local nineteenth-century historian, James Wilkins. He has a unique take on this area. I strongly recommend that you read it tonight.' He vanishes into the staffroom and shuts the door.

'Skerakis, what part of "starving to death" did you not understand?' Marlon asks pathetically.

'I suppose it didn't occur to you to take a shower? Why are boys so gross?' Bee's flared nostrils make her look like a fastidious deer.

'What did you expect?' I snap. 'I've been charging about a basketball court for sixty minutes. I would have showered, obviously, but I thought your royal snootiness was in a hurry.'

Then I remember that this girl is faced with the strong possibility that her old man is certifiably barking.

'I'm here, aren't I?' I mumble. 'Can we just go?'

It's dark outside and totally chucking it down. The street gleams with confusing reflections. We have to wait to cross at the lights. Bee looks unbelievably strained and I make feeble soothing noises.

'It'll work out. Trust me.'

'That's right, Dino! I've always got another dad knocking around somewhere if this one doesn't work out.'

Bee has this way of wrong-footing me that instantly makes me all huffy and defensive. 'I didn't mean – I was only trying to help!'

'Well, help in silence, OK?'

When we finally reach Mortagaine House, I summon the lift and we ride up to the top, still without saying a word. Then we ride back down.

'Want to try again?' I say in my huffy voice.

'Well, duh!'

'Gosh! Is that princess-speak for "yes"?' I say under my breath.

I lose count of the number of times we ride up, but each time we come down, I feel less of a hero and more like a right idiot.

'This is pointless,' I say at last.

'We haven't tried the service lift yet,' Bee says coldly. 'Remember Natz said someone heard it in the service lift?'

After another six trips, she looks so queasy, I decide to forget about my wounded pride.

'I'm calling an official tea-break,' I tell her. 'Come up and meet my dad. I'm serious. He'll be glad of the company.'

I think she's secretly relieved, because there's a sudden improvement in the atmosphere. As we get back into the passenger lift, she takes a deep breath and says shyly, 'I was sorry to hear about your dad's restaurant.'

So she had heard. Probably the whole school knows by now.

I put the usual positive spin on my family's depressing situation. 'Oh, Dad's cool. Reads all the job sections and everything. He's helping out at my uncle's restaurant for the time being. It's not permanent, just while he's looking.'

'Sure,' says Bee.

'Obviously it's not ideal. The taverna was like, my dad's life. He doesn't say, but I know he misses it. I think that's why he gets all these headaches. Plus the money thing.'

Bee nods sympathetically. 'Money is such a nightmare.'

I drag the lift gates into the closed position and press button 14. The round yellow eye lights up in the gloom. I'm suddenly aware of being all alone with her in a small enclosed space. I'd have expected Bee to use one of those designer fragrances. Something cool and astringent. But she smells like roses, that warm, slightly peppery smell they get in full sun.

It's just her shampoo, you muppet, I tell myself.

'So will I meet your mum?' Bee is still trying to be friendly.

The lift lurches into motion.

'No, she's at work. She manages that flower shop up near the hospital.'

'I know it! I had no idea your mum worked there. It's really classy.' Bee quickly covers her mouth. 'I didn't mean –'

I grin. 'That's OK. I think my mum is classy too.'

We make real eye contact for the first time.

This girl is *so* fit, I think. A split second later, the power cuts out.

We're stuck in the dark between floors twelve and fourteen.

My chest goes tight.

'This happens all the time,' I tell her breezily. 'You just have to keep pressing the button.'

I hit the button repeatedly. The lift stays where it is.

I squint up through the iron barrier. There's a giant step up to what I assume must be our landing. I start to haul at the gate.

'Don't, you'll fall!'

'No way, man! I'm an athlete.'

The gate opens so easily, it almost feels like someone is lending a helping hand. Wisps of dirty steam come curling into the lift.

Bee recoils. The stink is indescribable, sickly sweet and rotten; the kind that might come from an open grave.

'Old drains,' I tell her. 'This building is ancient. You should hear what my dad has to say about the wiring. Look, I'll give you a boost, then you can help me up.' I bend down so she can climb on to my back.

Bee goes dithery. 'What if I'm too heavy?'

'Just do it, woman!'

She clambers on my back and straightens up, giggling. 'Wouldn't it be weird if we'd found the thirteenth floor by accident?'

Bee slides off in a rush. She's wheezing like an asthma victim.

'Highly entertaining,' I tell her. 'Ha ha.'

She drags herself over to the panel, and starts frantically pressing buttons, still fighting for breath.

I feel a jolt of horror. She's not faking. There's something up there!

I grab her by the shoulders. 'What did you see?'

'Why won't the stupid thing *go*?' Bee moans.

The inside of my mouth has gone furry with fear but I have to see for myself. I make a grab for the edge of the landing above, pulling myself up, as if I'm doing a stunt on the parallel bars.

The air suddenly seems full of whispers. Swirls of vapour billow past. I take a breath and instantly choke. I don't know what it is, but it isn't steam. I'm straining my muscles to the max and my lungs are on fire, but I've *got* to see what she saw.

A clammy wind lifts the hair on my scalp. The fog rolls back and I find myself staring into a deeply disturbing interior. I almost said 'apartment', but that sounds normal. This has the sweaty yellowish glow you see in dreams. The walls are so slimy and encrusted, they seem unnaturally alive. The longer I look, the more nightmarish the walls become. I want to look away but I can't. The whispers become howls of suffering. The sound swells, filling my head, and it's like I'm listening to all the voices of every human being who ever suffered.

Out of this harrowing soundtrack, a new noise gradually makes itself heard. The eerie rattle of a small object rolling towards me. A pale shape comes spinning out of the murk. Something hairy and fibrous stealthily hooks itself around one of my fingers.

I yell out, trying to shake it off, but the thing is too firmly attached.

I go crashing back into the lift, whacking whatever it is against the sides of the lift, frantically trying to free myself. I fling myself at the lift panel and hammer all the buttons in turn. I think I'm moaning, maybe even praying, but I can't be sure. There's a sudden violent downward lurch. I make a wild grab for the lift gates and just manage to drag them across before it descends at breakneck speed.

For a few seconds we grate and groan our way down the lift shaft in total darkness. Then the light flickers back on and Bee sees the object swinging from my hand. She backs away. 'Oh my god, Dino!'

Fastened around my finger is a fraying filthy string. On the other end is a dayglo orange yo-yo.

CHAPTER 5

WE tear out of the front door so fast, I actually feel my trainers skidding on the greasy pavement. The street is slick and shiny with rain. The air is pure diesel fumes. A never-ending queue of cars, trucks and buses inches towards the traffic lights. It's rush hour.

Bee's voice is breathless with fear and running. I can't hear what she's telling me through the traffic sounds and I don't want to.

'I don't want to talk about it, OK?' I yell over my shoulder.

I'm gradually leaving her behind. I need to put as much distance between myself and Mortagaine House as possible, and I'd actually prefer it if Bee wasn't with me. I'd always sensed we were linked in some special way. Now it's like we share a disease.

I've got a murdered boy's yo-yo in my pocket. I've got a murdered boy's – I've got –

'This isn't just about YOU, Dino!'

Bee is shrieking at the top of her voice. She's just standing stock-still in the middle of the pavement, forcing disgruntled office workers to walk around her.

I make myself walk back. 'It's OK,' I tell her in my horse-whisperer voice. 'We had a weird experience, but we'll get over it and then it's going to be OK.'

Bee is almost beside herself. 'Will you *stop* saying that! Things will never be OK for us. Never *ever*.'

My heart turns over. 'What do you mean?'

'Open your eyes, Dino,' she says in a choked voice.

A girl brushes against me in the rain. Everything slows down and I see her in disturbing close-up. The glistening raindrops beading her face. Her glossy red raincoat. And the swirling darkness around her body.

I try to tell myself it's just a shadow. But shadows don't spark and burn like solar flares. Shadows don't –

I rub my eyes, desperate to make it go away.

'Tried that,' Bee says miserably. 'It doesn't work.'

The red-raincoat girl is chatting to her friend, laughing and gesturing. I watch them walk under a street light. Two girls, one flashing, flickering shadow.

A man with a briefcase hurries past and I go cold. I glance furtively down the street and count another four.

'I don't understand.' I try to control my voice.

'What's going on?'

Bee is trembling. 'Something weird. Something bad.'

'How long have you been able to –?'

'Since we left – your place.' Bee can't bring herself to say the name. 'I tried to tell you but you went zooming off. I'm scared, Dino.'

It's like a new mutant race. They're everywhere, coming out of the Metro store, buying evening papers at the kiosk, queuing at bus stops. One guy is talking loudly on his phone. I'd have taken him for your average city trader yesterday – expensive suit, major ego – but now I can see the telltale churning space around him. The man hails a cab and dives in, still talking. The taxi driver eases out into the flow of traffic, as nonchalantly as if he's carrying a normal passenger.

'Why is this happening?' I whisper.

'Maybe it's always been like this,' she says. 'Maybe we just couldn't see it until now.'

'You think we brought this back from the thirteenth floor, like some sick souvenir? The gift of evil shadows?'

'Dino, I don't *know*!'

'So why do only some people have them and others don't?' My voice is verging on hysterical.

She shakes her head. 'I don't know that either.'

A couple emerges from a hotel. They pause on the steps for a long kiss. Their shadows merge into one huge pulsating mass.

'I think something's happened to their souls,' Bee says in a small voice. 'Is that possible? Can you actually interfere with someone's soul?'

'I'm a basketball player,' I say angrily. 'Basketball players don't do souls.'

Even as I'm talking, I'm dragging her away. I don't exactly know what souls are, or even if they exist. If they do, that couple didn't have them. I saw their eyes and something was definitely missing. The crucial thing that makes you human; it wasn't there.

I can't say how long Bee and I walk in circles, trying not to look at anyone, trying not to think. We walk until we're literally shaking with exhaustion, but there's nowhere to go so we just keep walking.

We've seen into the city's dirtiest secret. We've seen all the ugliness it tries to hide; and now that darkness has followed us down into the city, and who's to say it won't follow us for ever?

'They can't be random,' I burst out. 'You wouldn't get one for no reason, surely?'

'I've got a theory,' Bee says in a strained voice. 'I think the shadow people took the lift up to – you know.'

'Then why haven't we got them?' I look down at myself in a panic. 'We haven't, have we?'

'Dino, I feel a bit –'

Bee suddenly turns completely pale. I grab her just before she falls. She doesn't completely faint but I can feel tiny tremors running through her.

'You need to sit down, Molloy,' I say firmly.

I drag her into the first café we pass, an internet place with stark halogen lighting. When I order two coffees, Bee unexpectedly revives and says, 'Actually, make mine a hot chocolate.'

'You want whipped cream? Marshmallow sprinkles?' asks the girl.

'I'll have anything going,' Bee says fiercely.

The girl laughs. 'The hell with the diet, eh?'

'What is it with women and diets?' I grumble, impersonating an average bloke, because right now my average-bloke routine feels like the only thing holding me together.

I carry our drinks past the rows of internet freaks. They look remote and otherworldly, clicking away at their keyboards, talking to their e-pals on the other side of the planet.

We sit down at a cramped metal table, and I knock back my espresso in one shot.

'You know what's weird?' Bee says. 'Part of me's in shock, but the rest of me's like, "Well, why are you surprised, Bee?"'

'Because of the legends?'

'Not just them. Didn't you ever have that feeling, Dino? As if life was meant to be lived in Technicolor but everyone's forgotten?'

I'm stunned. 'I'm – I'm not sure.'

'You know *The Wizard of Oz*? When the tornado blows Dorothy over the rainbow and everything explodes into colour? The first time I saw that movie I cried with pure relief! I was six years old, but I knew life wasn't meant to be lived in black and white.'

Memories stir deep inside me; so far down it feels dangerous. I didn't imagine it. Bee and I did have a connection, and we still do.

'I know what you mean,' I mumble.

I've got all these feelings churning inside, yet I sound like some tragic ape-man who got struck by lightning and accidentally acquired speech.

I clear my throat, trying to sound businesslike. Businesslike I can do.

'Remember that picture of Mortagaine House during the World Fair? I found another one, taken the month before. The thing is – the house wasn't there! Not a trace. Just public gardens or something.'

Bee's eyes grow wide. 'Remember how Tina used to tell us it just –'

'– in a ball of blue light. I know.'

She sniffs her drink with its bobbing pastel-coloured marshmallows. 'Tina used to say all the adults were hypnotised.'

I shake my head. 'That's all a bit *X-Files* for me.'

'Then how come people let our city get this bad?' She pushes her mug away, looking queasy. 'I can't drink this. I can't get that stink out of my head. Hope I don't have to go on smelling that place my whole life.'

'It's the soundtrack for me,' I say. 'Like souls being tortured.'

I instantly regret the reference to souls, but Bee isn't listening. She's staring in wide-eyed horror at the couple at the next table.

'Let me tell you, I'm going places,' the boy is saying to his overawed girlfriend. 'Got the BMW picked out already. By the time I'm twenty-five I'll have made my first million.'

We wouldn't have given him a second glance an hour ago. But it's not Romeo himself who has us mesmerised. It's all that manic pulsing and flashing, like some deeply sinister version of the Northern Lights.

'God, Dino,' Bee whispers. 'How can we go to school and act normal after this?'

I shake my head. 'I don't know.'

'If we could just tell someone –'

'Yeah, right! We'd look like those sad alien abductees.'

She gives me a wintry smile. 'I know. My mates kind of half-believe in the Mortagaine House stories, but they wouldn't want to think of them as being true.'

'Can you blame them? This thing is so huge. It makes you feel helpless, like a little kid.'

Bee stares at me. 'Dino, we weren't helpless when we were kids. We thought we could do anything!'

'We were wrong,' I say grimly.

'We weren't! Don't you remember that time at Halloween? We were telling scary stories under the table, and you told me you used to know how to do magic. You said you'd forgotten the rules –'

Memories come in a rush. Bad bazouki music on a

96

crackly sound system. The starchy smell of the tablecloth. Bee's wiry curls tickling my cheek as we shared Aunt Tippie's pastries, one syrupy bite at a time. That feeling of being ridiculously happy inside my own skin. These things I remember. But *magic*?

'You're mixing me up with someone else,' I tell her.

Bee's mouth sets in a stubborn line. Before she can argue, her mobile rings. From Bee's tone, it has to be her mother.

'I know. I *know*. I had to look something up in the library. Ask lover boy, if you don't believe me. This stupid project was *his* bright idea. I'm not being like anything. Oh, FORGET it!'

She puts her phone away, fuming. 'What is it with that woman? If we don't sit down together once a day and load up with unhealthy carbohydrates, my mother thinks civilisation will come to an end.'

I laugh. 'We should introduce her to my dad.'

One of the net freaks hurries past our table and accidentally kicks my bag. Waverley's book goes flying dramatically across the café. The decrepit cover finally parts company with the pages and they go fluttering everywhere.

Bee rescues the title page. 'Hey! What's a basketball

97

player doing reading *A Mystic's Life?*'

I shrug. 'Waverley told me to read it.'

'Any special reason, or just the usual Victor ego trip?'

'He threw a complete wobbly. Said James Wilkins had *unique* local knowledge and my report would be incomplete without it.'

I'm collecting up brittle brown-tinged pages, half expecting them to crumble like dead leaves.

'Ugh, footnotes,' says Bee. 'The only thing worse is graphs. No, maps! Maps are definitely –' she picks up the last page, 'worse,' she says in a different tone. 'Well, that is weird.' She peers closely at the sketch map. 'Dino, this is *ancient*.'

I fake a yawn. 'Sorry, I don't do maps either. Unless they have that lovely X to show you where to find the treasure. Anyway it can't be that ancient. The book was published in the nineteenth century.'

'The book is nineteenth century but the map shows the city like it was about a thousand years ago! There's a forest where my estate is, look! A medieval forest, Dino! They still had wolves back then, you know. Plus there'd be wild boar and charcoal burners and whatever.'

'Wow, charcoal burners!' Yet, against my will, I feel

a faint stirring of interest. 'So where they built Mortagaine House, that would have been forest too?'

'The whole country was forest then, just about, with tiny settlements dotted here and there. No matter where you lived in those days, the forest basically came up to your front door.'

Bee carefully flattens the map on the table, tracing a line with her finger. 'How bizarre! Look, this is roughly where Paris Gardens ought to be, but he calls it Paradise Gardens.'

'Ooh, how bizarre is that! A difference of three letters,' I mock.

'I know. The locals probably slurred their words and the name just got shortened. All the same, we should read it. It might help us understand what's going on.'

I grin at her. 'Who's an ace reporter now?'

Instead of retaliating, Bee hitches her chair across to my side of the table, and smiles expectantly. 'Well, go on!'

'You seriously want us to read this manky old book? Here and now?'

'Unless you're especially keen to rush home?'

I picture myself walking into the lobby of Mortagaine House and waiting for the lift. I imagine getting into the lift, pressing the button on the control panel and seeing it light up like a malevolent eye.

'Not especially keen,' I admit.

Bee briefly touches my hand. 'That's what I thought. You start.'

I start to read the intro in the 'OK, if I really have to' monotone I generally use for reading out loud.

'Master Ambrose Tully was a tenth-century merchant who became a monk and mystic, and founded a highly unconventional holy order on the site of the natural well where Monkwell Street is today. In the light of recent dark occurrences in this city, I decided to publish Master Tully's story at my own expense. It is my hope that his work will never be forgotten and that we may one day reclaim the lost wisdom that cost him so dearly.

'"Recent dark occurrences"?' I say uneasily. 'What's that about?'

Bee flips back. 'Dino, this was published in 1861!'

The year Mortagaine House first appeared.

We stare at each other.

Bee gestures impatiently. 'Keep reading.'

There's one problem, James Wilkins didn't exactly write his heavy-going Victorian prose with the MTV generation in mind, so as I read I'm also having to tease out the bare bones of the story, which basically boil down to this.

For years Ambrose Tully had earned a good living from trading in spices. By the time he reached his late thirties, he was a wealthy man. In those days, people didn't just buy spices to make food taste more interesting. They used them for medicines and preserving meat, and, more disturbingly, to disguise the taste of food that had already gone rank.

By medieval standards Ambrose had done well for himself. But when his beloved wife died giving birth to their son, life suddenly seemed meaningless. As months and years passed, Ambrose grew profoundly depressed. His state of mind became so dark that he genuinely saw no point in living. One morning, in total desperation, he fell upon his knees and prayed to be shown the way out of his suffering. His room filled with light and an angel –

I break off in disgust. 'Oh, give me a break!'

'Will you shut up and *read*?' says Bee.

'But it's complete crap! OK, OK!' I quickly scan the page and reel off a careless précis in a style that shows my opinion of this drivel.

'Erm, so his room filled with light and lo! an angel appeared. Ambrose's angel told him to go to a certain spot in the woods and dig down until he found a natural well with healing powers, as you do obviously. The angel said news of this well would spread and people would come from miles around to be cured of their unpleasant medieval ailments. The angel also foretold that this site would become the birthplace of a cosmic experiment – oh I LOVE this part – in which humans and angels would work together to create a second Eden.'

I roll my eyes at Bee. 'Victor reckons this guy had "unique local knowledge"? Unique local nutter, more like.'

She snatches the book away. '*I'll* do it then.'

Maybe it's her voice, surprisingly low for a girl's, or maybe it's easier to concentrate when someone else is weeding out the dull bits, but as I listen to James Wilkins' words filtered through Bee, the sounds of the café fade, and his outrageous story begins to work on my imagination.

The truly bizarre thing, to a modern cynic like me, is that Ambrose didn't doubt his experience for a second. He'd asked for a sign and BOSH an angel appeared! You got the impression earth and heaven were more in synch back then. Like, you just tugged your end of that invisible string and you'd feel Someone tugging reassuringly back.

Well, that's what Ambrose believed and it worked for him. He threw off his depression, fashioned a divining rod from a hazel twig, saddled his horse and rode off into the forest to locate the well.

He found it on the third day, minutes before the sun went down. There was no confusion about it being the right place. The moment the miraculous well water touched Ambrose's lips, he felt a shimmer of light enter his body and he was instantly cured of the suppurating mouth abscess that had bothered him for weeks. Having completed stage one of his divine task, Ambrose knocked up a rough shelter to keep off the wind and rain and waited for the rest of the prophecy to be fulfilled.

Everything happened as predicted. Men and women began to flock to the healing well and there were other even more miraculous cures. The blind regained their sight, the lame walked, and people who had lost all hope found new courage to go on living. Many were so stirred by the experience that they completely abandoned their old lives and stayed behind in the woods to help found a religious community.

Amongst these converts were beggars and outlaws, even thieves. One or two were regarded as harmless lunatics. Ambrose welcomed them all into his eccentric little order. They all took vows of obedience and poverty and camped out together in the woods: women as well as men, an arrangement seen as scandalous at the time.

The angel continued to visit Ambrose in the hour before dawn when everyone else was still sleeping. He had begun to instruct the former spice merchant in the use of what James Wilkins described as 'universal cosmic principles'. The angel warned Ambrose that these principles were so powerful that people might think he had stumbled upon the rules of magic . . .

Our eyes meet over the book.

I feel oddly light-headed, as if I'm coming unglued from normal time and space. If I turn round I might see –

I don't turn round. I take slow breaths and let Bee's voice draw me back into the story.

The angel explained to Ambrose that the mysterious phenomena which people of this time believed to be magic were really attributable to the natural laws which govern the cosmos. If humans followed these laws, the angel said, no one would ever be hungry, sick or afraid ever again. He asked Ambrose to write the teachings down, so this healing knowledge could be shared with others.

Soon the monks and nuns in Ambrose's order were applying these angelic principles to every aspect of their daily lives: from farming and brewing, to bee-keeping. The results amazed them. When they followed the angel's advice, things seemed to flow without struggle or effort. By the time the first snows came, the granary bulged with harvested grain and the monastery store rooms were overflowing with miraculous supplies of honey, ale and mead.

Most astonishing of all was the effect on the gardens, where vegetables flourished free from pests, and flowers grew that had never been seen before on northern shores.

I break into instant goosebumps.

'Paradise Gardens!' Bee whispers. 'Dino, can you believe this?'

Apparently I can. I'm surrounded by the crude concrete and glass of my own century but I'm seeing the glowing colours of miraculous medieval gardens. I can hear the bee-like murmur of tenth-century nuns and monks at prayer in their monastery among the trees. Ambrose Tully has suddenly become real.

Time passed. Months turned into a year, then two, and the original shelters of wattle and mud were gradually being replaced with buildings of stone. Ambrose's savings ran out during the construction of the library, but a sympathetic local nobleman chipped in and they were able to finish the work.

The angel still came every morning to dictate to Ambrose. And as soon as the library was finished, dedicated monks and nuns sat working from dawn till dusk, transforming Ambrose's scribbled notes into medieval calligraphy, decorating the margins with fine artwork in golds, blues, crimsons and greens. The angelic information was going to be bound into a book, the most wonderful book ever seen.

No one had set eyes on this angel, apart from Ambrose. Yet they never seemed to doubt that the spice merchant turned monk was in communication with a genuine celestial being. To them the making of this book was a holy task which would free the world from suffering. Their monastery would become a divine beacon, radiating heavenly light into the world.

But this wasn't heaven, it was earth, which in those days was something of a cosmic battleground apparently. It wasn't long before the phenomenally high levels of light pouring from the monastery attracted the attention of a being with a different – darker – agenda. James Wilkins seemed unwilling to describe this dark entity, and he flatly refused to use its name.

'This creature has fallen so far from the light, that I dare not say more for fear of conjuring it from the shadows as I write,' were his exact chilling words.

'NO way!' Bee desperately scans ahead.

'Hey, Molloy! Don't just leave me dangling!'

'Sorry, sorry.'

Bee reads on, increasingly distressed.

One night Ambrose dozed off at his desk. He woke with a start to find the candle burned down to a stub. It was midsummer but the temperature in his bare little cell had dropped to near freezing. Ambrose knew this creeping chill wasn't physical. He had been warned this might happen. He just hoped he had the courage and stamina to fight off his invisible visitor.

Suddenly he heard the voice he had always secretly dreaded, whispering into his ear. 'Stop and think about what you're doing, Master Tully,' it breathed. 'Stop this ridiculous collaboration with the heavenly realms and I'll give you power beyond your wildest dreams. Forget this little chapel in the woods! I'll build you a cathedral!'

'The realms of heaven are our true home,' said Ambrose. 'We came from there and to them we will all one day return. This book is the core of our work on earth. Without it the monastery would be meaningless.'

'That's just what the angel wants you to believe,' the voice said persuasively. 'But his book will bring humans nothing but pain. You know what they're like. They *think* they want to be free, but they're not ready for so much power, or so much responsibility. They don't want to know how the cosmos works. They like to have someone to blame when things go wrong. They want to be told what to do and when and where and how often to do it.'

'That's true,' Ambrose agreed. 'The human race is still only in its infancy. But children of the future will think differently. This book is for them.'

'Extremely commendable, I'm sure,' said the being sarcastically. 'But had you thought what will happen if news of this book gets out prematurely? If these angelic laws become common knowledge, people will accuse you of black magic. You and your precious book will be burned at the stake. You'd be much safer giving all your notes to me.'

'They aren't mine to give,' said Ambrose in a firm voice. 'I already told you. This book belongs to the children of the future.'

The stump of candle blew out, plunging the cell into pitch darkness. 'Maybe it's time someone showed you what these wonderful children are like,' hissed the voice.

Disturbing visions flickered over the bare walls. The green meadows and forests of Ambrose's time had vanished. High-rise towers of stone and glass blotted out the sun. Glittering machines droned through the skies, any one of them capable of vaporising a city at the touch of a button. Down below, humans scurried about like ants, lost in the shadows of their own creation.

Ambrose watched all this in distress, but he didn't say a word.

'You see how pointless your work is! The future is already in my hands!' gloated the voice.

'You're lying,' said Ambrose quietly. 'This book will help humans defend themselves against you and your kind. That's why you want it so badly. But you'll never get it, so you may as well leave now.'

A foul-smelling wind gusted through the cell, slamming the shutters against the wall and sending Ambrose's few belongings whirling through the dark. The monk tried to re-light his candle, but each time it blew out, so he knelt down in the whirling darkness and prayed for strength.

As suddenly as it had begun, the wind died down, and the voice spoke to Ambrose one last time. 'You're making a mistake, old man! Eternity is my playground. Time means nothing to my kind. But you have only a short time left on Earth. You can't protect your precious book when you are DEAD!'

And it was gone, leaving a rotting stench in the air . . .

Bee stops in the middle of the sentence. I don't tell her to go on. I don't want to see the connection between Ambrose's visitor and Jimmie Molloy's anonymous benefactor, but I don't seem to have a choice.

'We knew *something* was up there,' I say at last. 'It doesn't change a thing.'

She turns on me. 'Not for you! Your dad didn't sell your soul to get himself out of a jam.'

It's like that night at Daphne's all over again. Suddenly Bee's pain is everywhere like broken glass.

'Don't you get it? My dad, my *stupid* dad, tried to

trick this evil cosmic *thing* – and it's totally rebounded. It couldn't get me, so it's going to take Sadie's baby! Her unborn baby, Dino! And it's all my fault!' She buries her face. 'I ruin everything! I shouldn't even have been *born*!'

I don't know where the words come from, but I hear myself say in a calm voice, 'Sorry, Bee, we haven't got time for this. The important thing is to decide what we do next.'

I said 'we'. It just slipped out. What scares me is I think I meant it.

Bee looks stunned. She draws a long shuddery breath.

'Are you saying you'll help me?'

'I suppose I am, yeah,' I say offhandedly.

'The brave star basketball player is offering to go on a *quest*?'

This is something I'm learning about Bee. The instant her feelings get too hard to handle, she'll immediately try to offload them, by going on the offensive. Once you know this, though, it's easier to let it wash over you.

'Any chance we could go to your place to read the rest?'

Bee blows her nose on a raggy bit of tissue. 'I suppose.'

'Don't die of enthusiasm!'

'No, it makes sense. It's just – my mum can be a bit embarrassing.'

'Not a problem,' I tell her. 'I have embarrassing rellies of my own.'

I fish inside my coat for my mobile.

As usual my mother picks up.

'Hi, it's me. No, don't worry about food. I'll be late.'

CHAPTER 6

BEE'S estate is perched on a hill above the local flyover. The development is so new that all the trees still have plastic labels. The whoosh of traffic crashes against our eardrums as we hurry past raw-looking houses and apartments.

In an attempt to borrow charisma, the housing association has named the streets after dead poets. Bee and her mum live in William Blake Crescent.

'Blake saw angels,' Bee announces, as we turn into her street. 'His family thought he was nuts, not too surprisingly. I haven't read his stuff,' she says hastily. 'My mum looked him up when we moved here.'

You'd have to be one hell of a visionary to see angels in this street. Little kids are out on their bikes, circling aimlessly in the sickly glow of a lone street lamp. Bee's house is in a terrace of completely identical town houses.

'Jesus, Molloy, how do you know which is yours?'

She winces. 'Actually, it's not that hard.'

Bee points to an upstairs window. Vivid colours jump out. Pinks, golds and greens so vibrant, they literally pulsate.

'It's different,' I say.

'It's a visual nightmare. But you can't tell Mum.'

The Molloys might live in Legoland but I'm picking up a genuinely homey vibe. As Bee hunts for her key, I can hear mellow jazz playing upstairs and the clink of pots and pans. A gleaming lilac Clio is parked in front of the garage.

'I assume that's not Victor's.'

'It's Mum's, fool! Victor drives a clapped-out Fiesta.'

I follow Bee up to the first-floor living room: a multicoloured riot of ethnic hangings and sequinned cushions. Shelves overflow with paperbacks. More books are stacked on either side of the big saggy sofa.

I can hear Bee's mother talking softly in the next room.

'Don't say I didn't warn you,' sighs Bee.

We go through into the kitchen. Coming in from the raw autumn night, the light and warmth feel like heaven.

Music pours from a radio-cassette player. Bee's mum

is holding the phone in the crook of her neck, while she stirs a pan. 'I know it's your favourite. That's why I cooked it, fool! Yes, I'll save you some. Don't let the garage rob you. Yes, see you tomorrow. Mmm. Me too!'

She puts down the phone and narrows her eyes at her daughter. 'Finally made it home, eh?' She sees me hovering. 'Oh, hi!' she says in a different tone. 'Bee didn't say we had company!'

'This is my friend Dino,' says Bee. 'Can we stretch to one more?'

Claudette Molloy has a surprisingly sexy smile. Considering she's not Bee's biological mother, they're uncannily alike.

'It's always a pleasure to feed my daughter's friends. I don't often get the chance.' She gives me a speculative look. 'Haven't we met before somewhere, Dino?'

Bee quickly interrupts. 'So what happened to lover boy? It's not like him to pass up a free meal.'

'Bee, we agreed you'd stop calling him that.'

'Ooh, SORREE,' Bee says. 'What happened to *Victor*?'

'Car problems. He needs a new radiator.'

'A new car, more like.'

'Don't be mean. Fifi's a perfectly good car.'

'He calls his *car* "Fifi"?' I mouth to Bee.

She mimes sticking two fingers down her throat.

Claudette Molloy's face lights up. She's finally placed me. 'Didn't you two used to play with each other under the table at the taverna?'

The silence probably feels longer than it actually is.

Bee shakes her head in wonder. 'And you ask me why I don't bring friends home!'

Her mum just laughs. 'I could maybe have phrased that better,' she admits. 'Look, dinner will be another half-hour. Watch TV or something.'

'We could look that thing up on the net?' I hint to Bee. 'For Mr Waverley's project,' I add in a louder voice.

'Good idea,' says Bee equally loudly.

I follow her upstairs. As I step over the threshold into Bee's room, I have the sensation of passing through an invisible force-field. It's that different from the rest of the house. Cool colours, uncluttered surfaces. With its puffed-up pillows and wrinkle-free spread, Bee's bed looks as if it's been beamed straight from the pages of a lifestyle magazine.

She opens a closet and hangs up her jacket. Inside, clothes are stacked neatly on shelves or hanging in dry-cleaning bags.

My mouth drops open. 'You colour code your wardrobe!'

'I'm a control freak,' she says apologetically. 'Do you think I need help?'

I take in the desk with its tiny laptop, labelled box files, the tidy perspex in-tray, the typed list pinned to the notice-board headed THINGS TO DO.

'Actually, it's nice,' I say. 'My room still feels like a box factory.'

'Poor you. Moving house is so stressful.'

Bee puts a CD in the stereo. Undemanding chill-out music, just what I need.

I notice some polaroid snaps stuck to the back of her door. A girl in a leotard, striking breathtakingly lovely poses. 'This is you! I didn't know you were a dancer!' I narrow my eyes. 'Hey, you're busted, Molloy!'

Her cheekbones flush. 'It's not a secret. I just don't go on about it, that's all. But yeah, dance is sort of my passion.'

'That's what you want to be, eventually? A ballet dancer?'

Bee makes a face. 'No way. Can't take those dead swans! I'm a modern-dance girl. Anyway it's really the choreography side that interests me.'

'The control thing!' we say simultaneously.

We exchange startled glances, then laugh nervously.

I put on my Movietone voice. 'Meanwhile, back in the Dark Ages, a cosmic war is raging.'

Bee stares at me. 'That's it, isn't it? We're mixed up in some kind of cosmic war.'

'Bit one-sided for a war,' I object. 'Perhaps you hadn't noticed but angels don't drop by that often nowadays.'

'That's horrible,' she says. 'Like, you believe in unseen forces so long as they're dark? Is that what you think, Dino?'

Why is it girls get mad just because you don't see things their way?

I shake my head. 'I don't know what I think. Just read, all right?'

Bee takes up Ambrose's story where we left off.

Ambrose's night visitor was right about one thing. Ambrose didn't have long to live. He was an old man by medieval standards, almost forty-five. For years he'd suffered from an illness known as 'ague', the medieval name for malaria. Now the symptoms intensified, becoming disablingly severe. The monks tried the usual

118

herbal remedies, but soon Ambrose was too weak to leave his cell.

His invisible enemy had just been biding its time. Now the brothers and sisters of Ambrose's order also began to be afflicted with bizarre symptoms – boils, fits, violent vomiting – which no medicines could cure.

At mealtimes, plates, goblets, loaves of bread, and once an entire roast chicken flew through the air as though bewitched. Someone or something was subverting nature's most fundamental laws. With Ambrose out of action, the community became infected by a growing hysteria.

Monks and nuns began to panic. What if Ambrose's angel wasn't an angel after all? What if they'd been meddling with cosmic powers that were never actually intended for humans to use? Suppose they had unlocked a demonic box, and let unspeakably evil forces loose upon the world?

Everything began to fall apart. Followers left in droves. Ambrose was confined to bed by this time, but he sent reassuring messages to the brothers and sisters who remained. Their enemy could do them no harm, so long as they stayed focused on their holy task.

'These are dark times but unimaginably darker times

lie ahead,' he told them. 'And when they come, people will need our book more than ever.'

Ambrose became so frail that he was unable to hold a pen, and had to entrust one of the monks with the task of writing down the angel's teachings.

Before he found his way to the well in the woods, Will Burbage had been an outlaw, hiding out in the medieval forest with his fellow brigands, robbing unwary travellers. But these days he was a changed man.

Every day, before dawn, Will came to Ambrose's cell. Ambrose would repeat the words exactly as he received them from the invisible angel, and Will faithfully recorded them.

After months of work, this labour of love and faith was complete.

Will brought the bound manuscript for Ambrose's approval.

James Wilkins described the book as giving off 'an otherworldly radiance', which I picture as white light so pure that you can see all the other colours constantly changing within it. When Ambrose saw it he wept like a little child, because his life's work was done.

The moment was abruptly shattered by a warning blast on a horn. A mud-stained rider galloped into the courtyard. Monks and nuns came running to see what was wrong. 'Flee from this place!' he shouted. 'You've been betrayed. Soldiers are coming to arrest you for practising witchcraft!'

Ambrose was too ill to be moved, and Will Burbage insisted on staying with him. They would face their fate together. But the dying monk told him, 'My work is done. Yours has only just begun. Protect our work from harm and heaven will surely help you.'

Will couldn't disobey his master's last request. He bundled the book inside his monk's robes, saddled one of the monastery's horses and rode off into the forest.

Bee reads the last paragraph exactly as it was written by James Wilkins.

'Some say he went to find his old band of outlaws. They say that when Burbage showed them the book, the robbers fell to their knees in wonder, and vowed to protect it with their lives. What happened to the heavenly manuscript after that I am unable to say with any certainty. There are those who insist that it survives intact somewhere in the city, under the protection of an unknown guardian. But until I am able to read it for myself, I can only surmise what wisdom is contained within its pages. Meanwhile the Lord of Lies continues to live in our midst, and our city grows ever more shadowy by the hour.'

I close the book. ' "More shadowy by the hour",' I whisper.

The CD finishes. Neither of us moves. We just sit in silence until Bee's mother yells for us to come down and eat.

Downstairs, Bee listlessly pushes food around on her plate. She says she isn't hungry but I suspect she's still suffering side-effects from the thirteenth floor.

'I thought you were going out, Bee,' her mum says cheerfully, helping herself to rice. 'Someone's birthday, you said.'

Bee's cutlery clatters on to her plate. 'God! It's Monday!'

It's not surprising she forgot what day it was. I feel as if I've been through several lifetimes since we left school this afternoon.

But she's beside herself. 'I'm supposed to meet them at Legends. Roshelle's going to kill me.'

'You'll make it,' I mumble. 'You've got ages.'

'But I need to shower. I haven't even wrapped her present!'

I put down my fork. 'This is probably a bad time. I should go.'

Bee looks panic-stricken. 'Don't be stupid. At least finish your dinner!'

After the meal she drags me off to make coffee. 'You've got to come with me,' she hisses when we're alone. 'I can't do Legends on my own. Not tonight.'

'You seriously want me to come clubbing, dressed like this? Are you nuts! They'll never let me in.'

'They will,' she insists. 'You look fine.'

I give her a flirty grin. '"Fine" as in, "You sexy beast" or, "You could maybe scrape by if the bouncer is wearing a blindfold?"'

She scowls. 'I said you look OK! If you're fishing for compliments, you're out of luck.'

'Oh, now it's just "OK"?' I tease. 'I don't think looking "OK" is good enough to get me into Legends, do you? Anyway, I can't gatecrash your girls' night out. Your mates might think we're, you know, together.'

'They won't. I'll – I'll tell them you're gay.'

'Oh this just keeps getting better!'

Bee goes off to get herself ready, and I watch TV, while Bee's mum catches up on her case histories.

She glances over her reading glasses just in time to see fresh-faced American teenagers with crossbows beating back an evil demon. You can tell it's evil because, unlike the teenagers, it has a face full of oozing pustules.

'Do you seriously enjoy this kind of thing, Dino?' Claudette Molloy inquires in a baffled voice. 'Vampires, demons, unseen forces?'

I shrug. 'Not particularly. It's just something to watch.'

'All your generation seem fascinated by the supernatural.'

'It's because we've lost our moral centre.' I give her a cheeky grin. 'Personally I prefer the squishy ones with hazelnuts.'

She gives a surprised chuckle. 'Serves me right for talking like a social worker!'

Bee comes downstairs, looking illegally beautiful in leather trousers, halter-neck top and spiky heels. She looks appalled. 'Dino, please tell me you're not flirting with my mother!'

'I am *not* flirting!'

'You are. You've both got that little smirk.'

Her mum quickly talks over her, 'Got your taxi money, Bees?'

'Yes I've got my taxi money, and don't call me Bees. I'm not three.'

'Mobile?'

'Yes, I've got my mobile. *God!*' Suddenly Bee softens and gives her mother a quick kiss on the cheek. 'I'm a big girl, Mum, I can look after myself.'

'Maybe, but there are some funny people out there.'

'It's OK,' I say. 'We have crossbows.'

CHAPTER 7

THE weather's still foul outside. People's damp clothes turn the train rank and steamy. We lurch down tunnels, hurtling past forgotten turnings and abandoned stations, and all the time I'm forcing myself to stay calm. It's not just the breakneck speed, or even the suffocating weight of the city pressing down over our heads. I'm trying not to count shadows. I don't want to know how many there are. I don't want to think what that might mean.

Most of the shadow people look pleased with themselves, as if life is working out for them. What gets me is, even the lost lonely ones are going about their lives as normal, listening to their headsets, doing crosswords. How could you do anagrams at the epicentre of all that seething activity? How could you think? And Jesus, *how* would you sleep?

A woman comes to stand beside me, reading a newspaper, folded into a small precise square. Her shadow has smaller whorls of energy spinning inside it. It's a miniature galaxy in there! Once I start looking, I can't seem to tear my eyes away. I have a hideous thought. It *knows* I'm watching. The whorls spin faster. I feel a sickening sensation, a greedy tugging, as if something is being pulled from deep inside.

Bee quickly drags me down the carriage. 'You OK?'

I'm sick and trembling. Strap-hanging in a train full of shadows is much, much more terrifying when you know what they really are.

'Bee, they aren't shadows,' I hiss. 'They're more like – like, holes.'

'Holes?' she says blankly. 'Holes in *what*?'

'I think there's supposed to be something that stops our world from being contaminated with all the evil dross we've just seen tonight.'

People are starting to look at us. We're whispering like spies.

'I don't know what souls are, OK,' I say into her ear, 'but maybe if you take them away, it causes some kind of, you know, *vacuum*.'

Bee glances furtively at the woman with the paper.

'You could be right,' she mutters. 'But what are the holes for?'

'Pass. But just now I felt it trying to suck like, my – my *life* force, or something, out of my body.'

Bee darts another nervous glance. 'But she looks totally normal! They all do.'

'It's not them doing the sucking, is it? It's the billion-year-old vampire or whatever up on the thirteenth floor.'

Bee's eyes are suddenly almost all pupil.

'Dino, that's how it watches people. Through the holes! It could be watching us at this moment.' She has to press her hand to her mouth. 'It wants to take over the city! It didn't get the angel's book, so now it's taking over our city!'

The only sign that the black-painted door leads anywhere significant is the security outside. I've noticed that all bouncers have the same expression, verging on blank yet with the faintest sneer of contempt.

It's bizarre. Our world is in ruins, yet now I'm actually here outside Urban Legends, it's a matter of honour to get in.

I nod at the bouncer, and try to project limitless cool.

'Cheers, mate.'

Maybe it's a quiet night, because he just grunts and steps aside.

The club is at the end of a sharply sloping corridor. A thumping beat tingles up through my feet. The badly painted walls are scarred with graffiti. The corridor angles abruptly and we emerge into the thick purple twilight of Legends.

To my left is a massive gilt mirror reflecting everything in my immediate environment: purple Hammer Horror sofas, decadent squishy cushions with tassels, scruffy painted pillars. Everything except me.

Bee comes to stand beside me. She has no reflection either.

She's smiling. 'Everyone falls for it.'

It's not a mirror, just a very lifelike painting.

I fan myself. 'Thought I'd joined the ranks of the undead for a minute there!'

She laughs. 'Probably wasn't the best night for a first visit.'

'Probably not.'

The club's ambience is basically gothic with a touch of youth club tat. Bar staff wearing outsize crucifixes whizz up cocktails with names like Bloodsucker and Final Gasp. Over our heads iron candelabra drip candlewax. Clips from classic horror movies flicker across the walls. But I barely register these things. I'm already being pulled into the music.

A tiny Asian girl is crouching over the decks. One hand is pressed to her earphones, while the other makes minute adjustments to the rhythms pumping through the club. Her expression is rapt, but totally impersonal, as if she's receiving incoming data, beyond the normal human range.

God is a DJ, I think wistfully.

I read that on a T-shirt. That's how this girl DJ looks right now. Godlike. Drawing down the sounds of the universe, through the pure power of her concentration.

'That's Ninja Girl,' Bee yells. 'Do you like her?'

'She's all right,' I say. 'She's good.'

She darts a look from under her lashes. 'Don't you want to amaze me with your moves? Guys usually do.'

'Well, yeah, but I didn't want to overwhelm you straight off.'

'I'll take my chance,' she grins.

I let her drag me on to the dance floor.

This should be a dream come true. Beautiful girl, nice vibe. The ratio of shadows to humans isn't excessive. Yet I can't seem to get into my usual groove.

I'm not exactly sure who's dancing.

It's like that cheesy tablecloth trick Nikos, one of Dad's waiters, used to do to impress the customers. In one swift movement everything I thought I knew has been pulled out from under me. It's true that all the crockery is still in the same spot, but suddenly it doesn't look anything like so convincing.

The girl DJ is spinning a tune with a raw dark thudding bass. She starts to dance, lifting her face and hands to something we can't see, Wherever she is just now, you know it's got to be beautiful. All that messy personal stuff has been emptied out. She's beyond that. She can't be touched. She's a channel, a lightning rod for sound.

I wonder how it feels to be Ninja Girl, channelling cosmic vibes to earth, rearranging human molecules into new and better patterns.

'You'll never guess who's here!'

It's the second, maybe the third time Bee has had to yell over the music.

'Who?' Then I spot the gawky floppy-haired boy dancing with his eyes closed, and, like Bee, I can't believe my eyes. 'You think Tim Flowers could have a double?' I yell.

Bee mimes amazement. 'I know! Supergeek out clubbing!'

In our world of cool teenage mutants, Tim Flowers is the genetic throwback. With his eager-beaver expression, he could be a boy hero from an old children's annual. He even talks like a boy hero.

'He's not a *bad* dancer,' I say.

Not exactly bad, but not exactly natural either.

'Don't you think he looks just like Pinocchio?' Bee sniggers. 'We should kidnap him and give him a makeover! It'd be our good deed!'

'It looks like he's been kidnapped already. Who *are* those kids he's with?'

Whoever they are, they're pretty hard core. One actually has a tattoo on his naked skull.

Bee pulls a face. 'Actually, I think they're some of Victor's boys.'

'What's Tim doing, hanging out with them?' I wonder aloud.

She lets out a sudden shriek. Roshelle's posse has finally turned up.

'Hey, birthday girl! Where've you been?' Bee screams.

'We thought we'd check out the Bubble Bar,' Roshelle explains. 'Guess who we saw!'

Bee's friends have been rubbing shoulders with a TV soap celebrity.

'Bet she didn't look nearly as gorgeous as you!' Bee says.

Roshelle giggles. 'You're right! She looked *rough*, girl!'

They're like a flock of exotic birds, flapping and screaming. They keep up their shrieked conversation all through Ninja Girl's set.

Bee's managing fine on her own, if you ask me. But when I try to slip away, they won't hear of me leaving.

'You've got to dance with us all, Dino,' Natz tells me.

'*All* of us,' Persia stresses, 'or we'll get jealous.'

It's my all-time favourite fantasy: a bevy of gorgeous babes fussing and cooing over me. But there's nothing sexual about this attention, sadly. For some reason Bee's mates have simply made me an honorary chick for the night. Maybe she did tell them I was gay? As every guy knows, girls have a scary way of passing on info that only other girls can decode.

Natz is doing it now. 'She's had three, to *my* knowledge,' she hisses to Bee. 'When is she going to learn? She knows she totally hasn't got the head for it. Next thing she'll be, *you know*, with some total psycho.'

Bee shudders. 'That girl just has NO self-esteem.'

Ninja Girl leaves the platform and a live band comes on. Roshelle and Bee drag me off to dance. Without seeming to move, Tim gradually eases away from his mates. Next time I look, he and Persia are doing some really dirty dancing.

Roshelle fans herself frantically. 'I'm in shock! Supergeek has hormones!'

Natz's grin slowly fades. 'Who let them in?'

A gang of sharply dressed boys, black and white, has invaded the dance floor. It's not the high-octane dance style that makes everyone nervously clear a space. It's the vibe. People watch warily as the boys hurl themselves around the floor. Could be drugs, could just be high on their own testosterone. No one's quite sure, but everyone senses trouble.

Marlon likes to talk the talk, but with Marlon that's as far as it goes. These guys are the real thing.

Their leader saunters over to Persia and gives her a lazy smile.

'Baby, ditch this fool,' he says. 'You just *know* he can't give you what you need!'

Persia looks as if she's going to tell him to get lost, then she makes fatal eye-contact and Tim doesn't stand a chance. Like a seagull helplessly sucked into a jet engine, she lets herself be swept away.

'Later, Timmy!' she giggles.

Tim Flowers goes back to his mates. I see him shooting resentful looks at Persia's new admirer, as they dance hip to hip.

Between dances, the boy offers Persia swigs from his flask. She takes baby sips at first, but as the night goes on, I see her grab the flask, knocking the booze back in gulps. Next time I look, she's laughing so hard, she can hardly stand.

Bee and Natz go into a huddle. Bee says, 'I don't care if he's bloody Genghis Khan. I'm breaking this up.' She marches off.

I race after her to provide macho back-up if necessary.

I hear Bee say primly, 'My sister and I have to leave now.'

The boy gives her his sleepy smile. 'My girl's happy where she is, aren't you, India?'

'Persia,' she corrects muzzily.

'Whatever.' He lunges to kiss her.

Tim charges up, looking more like a boy hero than ever. 'I advise you to leave her alone.'

'Hey, it's Tintin!' laughs someone.

The skin round Tim's eyes goes unnaturally stretched. 'I *said*, I advise you to leave her alone!'

Persia's dance partner isn't smiling now. 'Little boy,' he says, 'you're making one BIG mistake.'

The other gang youths start to gather around. To my horror, Tim's mates start to gather around him!

'They're insane!' I tell Bee. 'These guys are sure to be tooled up.'

Bee's friends teeter over in their tight dresses and high heels.

'What's going on?' asks Roshelle anxiously.

'Don't let these fools spoil your party,' Bee tells her. 'We'll take care of it.'

Persia bursts into tears. 'I didn't mean to spoil Roshelle's party.'

Bee puts her arms around her. 'Ssh, sweetheart. No one said you did. Dino and I will take you home, won't we, Dino?'

'No problem,' I tell her.

The security guys are moving in. 'Take it outside, lads,' one says.

They hustle both groups out through the door.

'Are they going to hurt Timmy?' wails Persia.

'At least,' I say grimly. 'We'd better go after him.'

Bee and I struggle back up the sloping corridor, supporting her hysterical friend.

Outside, in the alley, both groups are staring each other down. For some reason Tim's mates now seem less sure they want to fight.

One hisses, 'You heard what Victor said. It's only for defence.'

'What do you call this – a party?' jeers the boy with the tattoo. 'If we don't do something, Tim's going to get hammered.'

'Not if he uses his head.'

'Right, like a battering ram!' says the tattooed kid. 'That'll work!'

'Run for it, man!' the first boy tells Tim. 'She's not worth it.'

Tim ignores his advice, looking worryingly serene for someone who's about to end the night in casualty. The boy with the tattoo grabs an old broom that's been dumped out with the trash and throws it to Tim.

'Catch!'

'What's he meant to do with that?' jeers the gang leader. 'Fly home to Mummy?'

Tim goes on smiling his disturbingly peaceful smile.

With no apparent effort, he snaps off the head of the broom.

It's rotten, I think. Only rotten wood breaks like that.

Tim begins to twirl the broken broom like a club. He's a different person. Calm, totally unhurried, absolutely focused.

The youths can't tell if Tim is incredibly courageous or off his head. Nor can I. The broom handle is twirling faster and faster.

'I've had enough of this!' says the leader in disgust. He reaches into his boot and I see the cold flash of a blade.

Tim moves so quickly I never really grasp what happens. In a bewildering blur of activity, he gets two with the broom, and while the third is gawking in shock, Tim catches him off balance and sends him slamming into the bins.

The youth slides down the wall and lies in a heap, moaning to himself.

The gang leader and his mate charge at Tim, yelling at the top of their lungs. Tim efficiently decks the gang leader's mate with the broom. This time it splinters, and he's left holding a useless stump – and the leader's still coming for him with the knife.

Tim whips round, grabs the dustbin lids and crashes them on either side of his head like cymbals. The boy drops like a stone.

Tim surveys the winded bodies calmly.

'Don't you EVER call me Tintin,' he tells them softly. Giving a last burning glance at Persia, he lopes away.

I'm stunned. 'What the hell kind of fighting style was that?'

Bee shrugs. 'Tai chi?'

'That wasn't like any tai chi I've ever seen.'

'Who cares? All fighting's stupid. Let's get Persia home.'

> *i know i acted like tim being a secret ninja was no big deal, it was b/c i was shocked, the fight was 2 much, on top of the evil shadows, i was dreaming all night, lost in spooky tunnels, running & running, then i woke up & i –*

Bee is sitting up in bed, swaddled in her duvet, peering at the tiny glowing screen in the lamplight. It's becoming a habit, writing rambling unsent texts to relieve her feelings. But this time it's not misery she wants to offload. She feels light-headed, literally dizzy with relief and excitement.

A murky dawn filters in through her window. Bee peers at the clock. At least an hour before he'll be up. Maybe if she can get the words straight in a text, she'll be able to say it right when they meet at school, face to face.

She shakily deletes the first message and starts a new one.

dino, i know how 2 save sadies baby

After last night, you wouldn't think I'd have any energy to dream. But I spend the remaining four or five hours of my night blundering through tunnels. Disturbingly trippy music keeps wafting towards me and I have to find the source before someone gets hurt.

When my alarm goes off I'm like the walking dead. Somehow I shower, dress, organise my school gear and make for the kitchen.

My dad is eating breakfast by himself, checking through his post. Mum's already gone off to the flower market. I spot a pack of painkillers propped against the marmalade, help myself, and gulp them down.

'You'll damage your liver taking those on an empty stomach,' Dad says. 'Have some toast. It's still hot.'

'Not for me, thanks. I'm running late.'

'How can you study if you don't eat?' Dad's face lights up. 'Why don't I fry you a couple of eggs?'

'Are you *deaf*? I'm late! I'm not going to eat six breakfasts just to give you an aim in life, OK?'

I slam out of the flat, pretending not to see his hurt expression.

Amazingly I make it in time for the first lesson. It's just an ordinary day, yet simply getting through it feels like the single most heroic thing I've ever done.

For some reason I've forgotten how to talk to my mates. I can't do that jokey blokey thing. Not today. Worse still, Marlon, Jude and the others seem to sense the change and back off, as if I've got some unpleasant rash.

Maths is followed by double English. The lessons are pure soundtrack to the mayhem playing in my head. I've decided to confront Waverley, ask him what he thought he was playing at, giving me Wilkins' book. I'm not going to let him fob me off this time. I'll keep

141

at him until he tells me everything he knows about Mortagaine House.

At lunchtime I march to the staffroom. Having psyched myself up, I'm not amused when it turns out Tuesday is Waverley's day for working with juvenile offenders.

I'm just on my way to the school canteen to refuel when I get a weird text from Bee, asking me to meet her in the music room. I didn't even know she had my mobile number.

I have to sprint to the opposite end of our school. I can see her through the open door, doodling chords on an electric piano.

'Dino!' When she hears me come in, she spins round. I can see she's all keyed up.

I close the door and for no reason suddenly feel trapped.

'How's it going?' I ask in an offhand voice.

'Oh, you know, a nightmare! But it's OK, because I've figured out what to do.'

'Well, that's good,' I say cautiously.

She takes a breath. 'Sadie came round to see Mum, while we were at Legends.'

'Any special reason?'

'I can guess. They probably had this big talk about how they should "involve" me with the new baby, like I'm two or something! The point is, Sadie left this.'

From the way Bee handles the small card, I can tell it's supposed to be special. Sadie's name and address are printed on the front, with the name and phone number of the local hospital. Inside, someone has glued a swirly little photograph of – who knows what?

'It's from her scan!' explains Bee.

When I finally decode the swirls, there's a tiny space alien with a bulging forehead and jellyfish limbs.

'It's a baby,' I say without enthusiasm.

Bee laughs. 'That's my little sister, excuse me! See, how she's sucking her thumb!'

'I'll have to take your word for that.'

'Isn't it the weirdest coincidence that Sadie suddenly decided to bring this round to our house last night? Dino, this is going to sound crazy, but I keep feeling this is like, our *destiny* or something! God! It's like you *knew* about that angel book, even back when we were little kids. "The rules of magic." That's literally what you said!'

I give her the card back. 'I told you that wasn't me.'

I'm not just feeling trapped. I'm suffocating.

OK, I admit it. When I agreed to go up to the thirteenth floor, I was just playing at heroes. I had no idea what I was letting myself in for. But now I know better, and I'm sorry, I just can't be Bee's knight in shining armour. She's got a picture of us in her head: the childhood sweethearts who grew up to wage war on evil. But this is based on a memory of an earlier Dino. A person who no longer exists. The kid who played under tables and chatted about magic. Conversations I don't actually freaking remember!

She's watching me expectantly.

'Sorry? What was that?'

'Dino, it's so obvious! We've got to find the book! It's the only way we can save Sadie's baby.'

She's smiling, as if she's come up with the perfect solution to a world shot full of holes.

I stare at her. 'The book? The *angel's* book?'

'I know! I don't know why we didn't think of it right away.'

'And after we've found it, what then?'

Bee doesn't notice the edge to my voice.

'I don't know. Maybe there's something about how to cancel supernatural contracts. I just know we've got to find the book, that's all.'

'That's all,' I echo. 'That seems like quite a lot.'

'We can do it, I know we can!' Her eyes are shining.

How is this happening? How did a foggy little snap of a tiny unformed being turn Bee into a believer overnight? She's gone skipping off into some fuzzy rainbow world of crystal kisses and amazing co-incidences, and just naturally assumes I'll follow.

'I don't know, Bee,' I say helplessly. 'Don't you think we're getting a bit out of our depth?'

Her face crumples. 'You don't *know*? You said you'd help me.'

'I will. I mean, I want to. I just – Isn't this a bit desperate? Looking for a book allegedly dictated by an angel, almost a thousand years ago?'

Bee thrusts the photo into my face. The force behind her words almost knocks me off my feet.

'Yes, it is desperate, Dino. This is my little sister, who is also out of her depth, might I point out. She's totally innocent, but she's got this evil threat hanging over her. Who'll save her if we don't? My dad?' Her voice cracks. 'Yeah, that'll happen.'

'I suppose if you put it –'

'We're all she's got, Dino! We're her only hope in this world.'

I look at the picture of Sadie's baby, then I look at Bee, her face ablaze with her holy mission.

Skerakis, you are in *such* deep shit, I think.

'OK, I'll meet you after basketball,' I say reluctantly.

The changing room smells of boys' sweat and trainers.

My former mates roar with laddish laughter, making a point of excluding me.

Marlon and Jude have been my mates for ever. If you'd asked me what they were like before today, I'd have said they were sound, safe, a good laugh. Now I don't seem to know who they are. It's like being friends with them was just a habit.

Jude and Marlon start play-whipping each other with towels, and I have a disturbing insight. They're *acting*! They get up every morning, put on their twenty-first-century costumes and assume their twenty-first-century laddish personalities.

And you know what? I truly envy them for being able to kid around, while everything that is good and human about this city leaks out through a billion black holes.

They're living inside an illusion, but my former friends don't know that, so they feel utterly secure.

But my old world has evaporated, taking me with it. 'How will we go to school and be normal?' Bee asked in the café. Now I know the answer. We'll never be normal again.

Will I feel this lonely for the rest of my life? Is there any way out of this nightmare that isn't going to hurt?

Through my fog of self-pity, I remember that I haven't eaten since yesterday. I have a not very reliable memory of leaving a Snickers bar in my locker. I fumble for my key and turn it in the lock. But as the door swings open, I forget all about my need for empty calories.

There's a parcel in my locker.

There's no way I can rationally know it's the angel's book. Wrapped in its layers of brown paper, the bulky shape could be anything. An atlas. A photograph album.

But as I tear off the wrappings, my hands go as weak as a newborn's. I notice every detail with brilliant clarity the way you do in dreams. The buff-coloured leather, fine and warm as skin. The stiff, unevenly golden edges of the pages, which give the impression the manuscript inside has been dipped in liquid gold. Its peculiar weight, which somehow seems more than pure physical bulk. Like I'm literally feeling vibes from the supernatural data inside. On the spine are two foreign words hand-lettered in gold leaf: *Liber Lucis*.

Logically, there is no way I could be holding a lost work of angelic wisdom in my hands. James Wilkins' book has practically disintegrated after only two hundred years. The angel's manuscript would have to be at least eight centuries old. Yet this book is completely intact.

But the words on the binding, I'm almost sure they're in Latin. Wasn't that the language medieval people used whenever they had to write something important? It is the lost book. It has to be. All at once my heart is banging against my ribs like a door in a gale, going, *Open it! Open it!*

I open the book and everything goes out of focus – sound as well as vision. The clangs and scuffles of the locker room blur around me. The air fills with a more distilled version of the smell in Mum's flower shop, and the intense springtime vibe that goes with that. Impossibly I hear outdoor sounds: invisible birds, a soft breeze, murmuring water.

My hands shake as I turn to the title page, and find the same mysterious foreign words. I can feel my heart jumping in my chest as I flip to the next page.

Nothing. Just a flawless gold-edged page.

I turn the pages more quickly. I turn them faster and faster until they blur before my eyes, and every one is blank.

CHAPTER 8

PLAYING basketball is a lot like DJ-ing. In both cases, you have to get in the mix. You've got to really feel it. It's like you connect to something invisible. If you do it right the music, or the game, will play through you. But not today.

I'm rushing round the gym, dodging this way and that, trying to grab the ball, but my mind is all over the place.

The book in my locker clearly has everything to do with the events of the last few days. But who put it there? And why?

I don't even have solid proof that this *is* the angel's book. I can't read Latin. For all I know *Liber Lucis* is ancient Roman for caffe latte.

The ball zips past my ear with an audible *whoosh*! At long last my basketball gene kicks in. I launch myself into the air. It's mine! I'm running like a madman, bouncing the ball, tantalising the opposition.

As I make for the net, I have a brainwave. Tim Flowers! I bet he dreams in dead languages.

Out of sheer high spirits, I aim the ball and throw, an act of total insanity from where I'm standing. Everyone gawks, wondering what's got into me. The ball teeters on the rim then, by divine fluke, drops through the net. I yell with triumph. It's a sign!

When basketball practice is over, I text Bee to tell her there's a change of plan. Why don't I tell her what I'm up to? I'm not sure. Maybe I'm a talking ape-man after all. Maybe I wanted to drop my find in her lap like a hunter returning from the chase.

Hey, baby! I've brought you the secret laws of the universe. Yeah, I had them translated into twenty-first-century English. Together we'll make the world safe for humankind!

Then again, maybe I just want to punish her for landing me in this mess. Whatever, I rush off to the school library.

I never doubt for a moment that Tim will be there. The library is Supergeek's little home-from-home.

Sure enough, he's over by the window, copying complicated-looking formulae into an exercise book. He flushes to his ears when he sees me. 'I just want to

151

say I had absolutely no idea Persia was your girlfriend,' he says stiffly.

I shake my head. 'Don't know who you've been talking to, but they're having you on. Persia is not my girlfriend.'

Tim looks confused. 'So why did you rush after me last night?'

'Thought you needed back-up. Obviously you didn't. That was some show you put on.'

'I have a good teacher,' he mumbles.

I rudely talk over him. 'Correct me if I'm wrong, but pointless information *is* your thing, isn't it, Flowers?' I place the book in front of him so he can see the spine. 'Any idea what this says?'

Tim goes absolutely still. 'Where did you find it?'

'It turned up in my locker.'

'No, seriously. How did you get hold of it?'

'I told you, it just turned up. Now I need you to tell me what this says. You do know Latin?'

'*The Book of Light*,' he whispers. He hardly has to look; it's like he already knew what he was going to see. He glances round to make sure no one is watching. 'I can't believe you've got this. May I?'

Tim tremulously opens the book. The scent of

invisible flowers wafts through the air. Invisible birds sing. The librarian looks up in surprise. Then it's gone and there's just the sound of Tim flicking frantically through the stiff parchment pages.

'Don't bother. They're all blank. I checked.'

The library has gone back to sounding and smelling like a school library. At the next table two girls giggle over a text message.

When Tim is disappointed, he droops like an old man. He pushes the book back across the table. 'You should give this to Victor Waverley,' he says in the voice well-behaved people use in libraries.

'Why would I want to do that?'

'It would be wise,' he insists.

'You're very pally with Waverley, aren't you?'

I suddenly get it. Tim must be one of Waverley's youth club kids.

'You should take it to him,' he repeats stubbornly. 'I'm serious. You have no idea what you're getting into.'

'Ooh, you're right! After all, I can't do tai chi like you, Timmy.'

Tim flushes. 'No need to be offensive.'

He ducks his head and carries on scribbling.

'That's it? That's all you're going to say?'

'You asked me what the title meant. I told you,' he says without looking up. 'If you want to know any more, ask Mr Waverley.'

'I don't think Bee Molloy would go for that!'

Tim's pen stops moving. 'You didn't say she was mixed up in this.' With his big helpless eyes, he looks like a worried spaniel.

I've never thought of myself as a bully, but Tim's pathetic vulnerability, mixed with the way he mysteriously hints at inside knowledge, makes me want to kick him hard. I have a sudden impulse to show him I have inside knowledge too.

'Yeah, you know how it is, her dad did a deal with a supernatural being and now her baby sister's got to pay,' I reel off carelessly, 'which you've got to admit is kind of unfair as the kid's not actually born yet.' I jam my hands in my pockets. 'Oh, well, gotta run, sorry to interrupt your important algebra or whatever.'

Tim is scribbling again. He tears a corner off his pad and shoves it into my hand. 'I'm going home in a few minutes. That's my phone number in case you need it.'

'Yeah, that'll happen,' I say scornfully.

'It's trigonometry, actually, not algebra!' he calls after me.

I stroll out, doing my hard man's walk. But I'm disgusted with myself. I should never have blurted out Bee's personal business like that. That was uncalled for. That was low.

Outside, it's that cold greenish twilight you get on winter afternoons before it goes totally dark. The air smells of burning leaves and car fumes. At the traffic lights, the same drunk is roaring at passers-by. 'It's too high. The price is too high!'

'Go to Asda, fool,' someone jokes.

My phone plays a perky tune. It'll be Bee, wanting to know where I've got to. I don't take the call. I'm watching the old man bellowing at everyone that crosses his path. Could that ever be me? Could I end up ranting at strangers on the street? Could my mind spin off into hyperspace for no reason and start downloading secret messages from the Venusian thought police? I turn cold. What if it's already happening?

The traffic lights change, but I can't move.

I'm staring at that sad old lush, as he goes on acting out some drama in his head, but I'm seeing me and Bee, tearing out of Mortagaine House, off our heads with hysteria. I'm seeing us on the tube, wild-eyed and babbling about a nameless evil. Behaviour so far left of

155

normal that normal people would call us deranged.

The more I think about it, the more insane our behaviour seems.

So the lift jammed between floors. But what did we *see*, apart from evil-smelling steam, plus gruesome brick-work? OK, the yo-yo incident could take some explaining. That orange plastic yo-yo is indisputably real. I left it in my room amongst the packing cases and dirty washing, while I figure out what the hell to do with it. Sure, finding Martin Coombs' yo-yo was a weird coincidence, but, to normal people, weird is not the same as meaningful.

But the book? And those woodlands FX? asks the voice in my head.

A book which turned out to be completely blank, my logical self points out. My hyperactive imagination supplied the rest. That's what the brain does; it generates pretty patterns out of random events – or, to put it another way, urban legends out of dross.

I grope my way to a wall. I've been saved by the skin of my teeth, and the head-rush of pure relief has made me see stars.

FACT. I never noticed the black holes until Bee pointed them out! OK, the black hole theory was mine. But it was fuelled by her paranoia.

FACT. It was Bee's delusion, from day one. But I forgot my own rules and got sucked into the whole crazy evil-bargain scenario.

I don't blame Bee. You don't need a degree in psychiatry to see she has problems. It's got to affect you, hasn't it, being taken away from your mother at birth, then having your second set of parents split like that? It's bound to make you wonder if it's you.

Now her dad's having his first real kid, his own flesh and blood. Plus her mother's new boyfriend, a man Bee loathes and despises, comes and stirs everything up. It's not surprising she's lost the plot.

It's like being released from an evil spell. I start to make for home at a run. I feel light and free, as if some crushing weight has been lifted off my shoulders. FACT. There is no malevolent all-seeing being sapping the city's life force from the thirteenth floor. FACT. There IS no thirteenth floor!

I'm back in the real world where I belong! No more brooding. No more sleepless nights. I swing in through the lobby, take the lift up to the fourteenth floor without a second thought, and let myself into the flat.

My parents have been busy while I've been away. The living room looks genuinely homey. In the kitchen, Mum's giving first aid to a bunch of red roses which have officially passed their sell-by date. Dad is spreading gooey frosting inch-thick on a huge chocolate cake.

'Nice!' I say appreciatively. 'What are we celebrating?'

'Helen and Mike are coming over with the kids,' Mum explains.

The bell rings a few minutes later. Dad opens the door, and we hear desolate catlike yowls.

My cousin Helen plonks a screaming baby in Dad's arms. 'Take him!' she laughs. 'No, I mean it, keep him for ever! He kept that up all the way over in the car. Mmm, I smell chocolate cake!' She plonks a bottle in my hand. 'Pop this in the fridge,' she says. 'Little housewarming pressie.'

Katinka hurls herself at my knees. 'Dino, Dino, Dino!'

My cousin recently started allowing Katinka to dress herself. Today she's wearing a grimy fairy dress with a matching crown, a striped blue and purple scarf, scarlet tights and flamingo-pink welly boots with built-in sparkles.

'Great outfit, Kittycat,' I tell her. 'This girl will have

her own designer label by the time she's five,' I whisper to Helen.

She grins. 'Have you seen the state of that dress! She'd wear it in bed if I let her.'

Dad is showing the baby its reflection in a sitting-room mirror. It gives a surprised chuckle. 'That's right, my darling, it's you,' says Dad. My father has a way with babies. He and Mum wanted loads, but it didn't work out.

'Mike didn't come with you?' my father calls.

'No, he did. He's just looking for somewhere to park.' My cousin wanders over to the window. 'This is a great place, you guys. Amazing views!'

'This is a real fairy crown,' Katinka tells me solemnly. 'It's quite magical, don't you think?'

'Extremely magical. So what happened to your wand, Kittycat?'

She shoots a dark look at Helen. 'My mummy made me leave it at home.'

'She kept poking her baby brother,' Helen explains.

'I was only trying to turn him into a frog,' says Katinka indignantly. 'What's so wrong with that?'

'Yeah, Helen,' I say.

Mike comes puffing into the flat. I hear him dump

something heavy behind me. He bangs me on the back. 'Dino! How're you doing?'

I turn to smile. Suddenly every tiny detail stands out: the white shirt straining across Mike's chest, gold rings glinting on pudgy knuckles. The seething darkness around his head and shoulders . . .

'I'm doing OK,' I croak. 'We're settling in OK.'

'Excellent! Always nice to see good people land on their feet. What about these views! Aren't they something?'

Dad comes over and pumps his hand. 'Mike! Congratulations on the new job. You must have impressed them.'

'Yep, finally got lucky.' Mike plumps himself down on the sofa. 'You wouldn't believe the perks, Kostos! Free health insurance, company car. And the bonuses are astronomical.' He taps his nose. 'A little girl I know just *might* be getting that trip to Disney World!'

Katinka clambers on his knee and nestles against his chest.

'Aah, who's a daddy's girl?' coos my mum.

'Tinker's my little mate, aren't you?'

Mike strokes Katinka's smooth glossy hair.

My parents see a solid human hand with stubby

knuckles and gold signet rings. They don't see the other shadowy fingers hovering over his little girl's hair. They don't know Mike isn't in control.

I make a sick strangled sound and bolt from the room. Startled voices follow me.

'What brought that on?'

'Who knows what goes on in their heads?' sighs Mum.

'Hormones,' Mike laughs. 'I remember them well!'

'That's no excuse for the boy to forget his manners.'

I lean against my closed door, trembling, remembering something I overheard our priest telling Dad. 'You know the devil's greatest triumph, Kostos? It made us believe evil doesn't exist.'

I used to look up to Mike. I used to want to be just like him. The thought makes me want to throw up.

I fish the crumpled piece of paper out of my pocket, and punch the number into my phone. 'Get down here right now, Flowers,' I say harshly. 'There's something I need you to see.'

CHAPTER 9

TIM lopes into the lobby, Boy's Annual hair flopping in his eyes.

'Sorry if you had plans,' I say offhandedly.

He looks shy. 'It's fine. It's on my way to youth club. What did you want to show me?'

'It's not the kind of thing you can explain.'

Tim follows me into the lift like a puzzled puppy. I press the button.

'It'll probably take a few trial runs.'

Tim goes white. 'You're not seriously –?'

'Yes I am. And so are you, boy genius.'

Tim barges out just as the doors close. To my annoyance, I'm forced to go after him.

'You're not chicken?' I taunt. 'A hard street-fighter like yourself?'

'No, I'm not chicken,' he says stiffly. 'I'm nervous, of course. But mostly I'm up to here with all those "boy genius" cracks.'

It's his dignity that gets me. Marlon and Jude at least get to choose the parts they play. But Tim Flowers didn't choose supergeek. We did that, the popular kids. We clocked the haircut and the retro vocabulary, factored in that eager-puppy expression and decided that's who he was.

I take a breath. 'Could we just rewind? I've been having a bad day, but I shouldn't take it out on you. Come with me, please. It's important.'

He flushes. 'Why me? Why not ask one of your real mates?'

'Assuming I even know who my real mates are, I don't think they'd have the first idea what we're up against.'

He gives me a funny little smile. 'The question is, do you?'

'I think I'm beginning to. So, are you on?'

Tim reluctantly gets back into the lift.

'Thanks, man,' I tell him.

He pulls the gate across, obviously uneasy. After the usual delay, the cage begins to creak laboriously upwards. We judder from floor to floor. This time there's no need for trial runs. As we go past the twelfth landing, the light goes out with an audible *ping*! and the lift stops between floors.

It's expecting us.

I can see the whites of Tim's eyes in the dusk.

'Is this it?' he says hoarsely. 'Is this the thirteenth floor?'

'I'm not sure.'

The only sound is our breathing in the confined space.

The air seems normal. No toxic fog, no smell of rot and decay, only a surprise whiff of antiseptic. Perhaps this *isn't* the thirteenth floor. In the real world, lifts break down all the time for perfectly logical reasons.

'Give us a boost and I'll check it out,' I tell Tim.

'I'll go first,' he shivers. 'I'd rather see what I'm in for.'

'Sure, whatever.'

Tim scrambles on to my back, hoists himself up and disappears.

I wait for exclamations of horror.

'You OK?' I call anxiously.

'Yeah.' Tim's voice sounds strangely echoey.

'What's it like?'

'See for yourself.'

His head and shoulders reappear. Tim's martial arts training seems to have made him phenomenally strong. He pulls me up with absolutely no signs of effort. But as

I scramble to my feet, everything else leaves my mind.

I'm looking down a pristine white corridor. On my right is a row of closed doors, all painted gleaming white. On my left, blue-tinted glass windows reach from floor to ceiling.

This place bears no resemblance to the slimy lair of my previous visit. It isn't just clean, it's sterile. I walk over to the windows to check the view. It's the usual dockland cityscape of warehouses and cranes, but the tinted glass makes it seem peculiarly dreamlike and far away.

We walk cautiously down the corridor. It's so quiet I can hear the squeak of Tim's trainers on the polished floor. The doors have an expensive satiny sheen. Each door has a peephole of tinted glass.

I peer through one but there's just a tinted reflection of my own face peering back. I try to turn the handle but it's locked. Tim tries the next one along. That's locked too.

We try door after door after door. The silent gleaming corridor and its mysterious sealed rooms seem to go on for ever. I find myself remembering a story Aunt Tippie told me when I was small.

A young girl marries a lord. He's charming and

good-looking but his beard seems suspiciously blue in a certain light.

The lord tells her she's free to explore every room in his castle, except the locked chamber at the top of the tower. But the minute he leaves the castle, she goes creeping up the stairs and unlocks the forbidden door. Inside are all the mutilated blood-soaked bodies of all her husband's previous wives.

These are offices, Dino, I tell myself. Normal twenty-first-century corporate offices. To my relief the never-ending corridor eventually comes to an end.

As we reach the last door, I notice a printed plaque. We both stare at it as if it might explode.

'Why would anyone put your name on a door?' Tim whispers.

I swallow. 'Let's find out.'

I wrench at the handle, which instantly gives way. Taken by surprise, I stagger into the room on the other side. Before Tim can follow, a gust of antiseptic-smelling wind slams the door in his face. I go to let him in but there's no handle.

I can see Tim through the peephole, looking worryingly far away, yelling and pounding on the door.

'Hold on!' I yell, as if Tim's in trouble, not me.

A pumping beat starts up, drowning out the sound of his shouts.

I get a deeply creepy feeling in between my shoulder blades.

I *know* this bass line. These are the trippy rhythms that keep me awake in the small hours. The music was coming from *inside* Mortagaine House the whole time.

A surging ocean of sound washes in over the beat. It's not the sea, it's wave upon wave of voices, euphorically chanting just one word over and over. I spin in shock. They're calling my name!

There's an explosion of noise: clapping, stomping, whistling.

'I can't believe he's here!' someone screams.

I'm in a club, the kind I've only ever seen in movies. Everyone drips effortless understated style.

I'm quite well up on the local music scene, but I've never *heard* of a club in Mortagaine House. And how come these people know me? Not just know, it's like they absolutely *worship* me.

Ecstatic girls stretch out their hands, pleading tearfully for me to notice them. The males just stomp their feet, and chant faster and faster, 'Dino! Dino! Dino!' Multicoloured laser-beams swoop and criss-cross.

The crowd surges forward. I find myself being helplessly carried towards the DJ platform.

'Go on!' a voice urges in my ear.

I'm in danger of being trampled to death, so I shakily climb the steps.

The DJ takes off his headphones, visibly relieved. 'Where've you been, Dino, man? I tried to keep them warm for you.'

'The headphones?' I say stupidly.

'The kids, fool! They've been going crazy! You're the star attraction!' The DJ knocks my knuckles respectfully. 'Keep it real, bredren, yeah?' he grins.

He vanishes, leaving me alone in the spotlight.

With some people it's fast cars or sex. For me it's music. Suddenly this small overheated booth smells of everything I've ever wanted. I want it so much, it's like vertigo.

Then I see the titles on the neat stacks of vinyl. My mouth just opens and closes without a sound. These are the tunes I picked out for my DJ set. The exact tunes.

The sound of my name is still crashing against my eardrums.

'Dino! Dino! Dino!' Each fresh wave gives me goose-bumps. Is this how it feels? Is this really how it

168

feels to *be* someone?

I peer over the bobbing heads in complete bewilderment. I can't seem to remember how I got in. Each time I almost locate a door, an exuberant fan blocks my view.

I want to believe this is really happening, but I have the feeling that crucial information is missing. Everything is a blank until I walked into this club; as if I wasn't born until the moment I heard everyone calling my name.

Should I go for it? Just play along, put on the headphones, and give these kids what they want? Could I actually pull it off, though? DJ-ing in my state of amnesia seems a risky proposition. Everything is so confusing. The lights, the noise, the increasingly restive crowd.

'Don't say basketball players get stage fright?' says an amused voice. Bee joins me in the tiny booth.

I'm amazed. 'How – how did you –?'

I want to ask how she knew I'd be here, when I didn't know myself. But it seems unusually hard to form words.

'You don't think I'd miss my boyfriend's big night?' Bee places her finger lightly on my lips. My insides instantly turn to melted caramel. 'Now, no more questions,' she says softly. 'Just go with the flow.'

Bee's clingy top and jeans exude effortless cool. We're like those young celebrities you read about in magazines; DJ Dino and his gorgeous girlfriend Bee Molloy. We're the golden couple all these kids secretly want to be.

I want to go with the flow like Bee says, I really do. I just can't.

'Not right!' I force out. 'Got to save – urgh! Baby.'

The sentence takes every ounce of concentration, and I still sound like a lightning-struck ape.

Bee's eyes go wide with sympathy. 'This is all my fault, you poor thing! I can admit it now. I think I really was jealous of Dad having a new kid. But I shouldn't have dragged you into it. I'm so sorry.'

I'm having huge complicated thoughts, but I can't seem to pin them down. 'Didn't drag me!' I say furiously. 'Wanted – WANT to – help!'

'I know, and I'm grateful,' she says in a soothing voice. 'I needed someone and you were there for me. But this is *your* time, Dino. This is your big DJ debut. You've got to put all that other stuff out of your mind.'

'No, no, NO!' I howl. 'Your dad made – a DEAL!'

170

'Babe, you're trying to be kind but we both know my old man has finally lost it.' She lets out a little spurt of laughter. 'I almost lost it myself! But I've moved on and so must you. Life doesn't have to be one big struggle, hon. It can be fun.' She's getting closer now, moving her body subtly to the beat. 'Isn't this fun, Dino? Isn't this the night you've always dreamed of?'

The spotlight gives Bee's skin a rosy glow like a peach.

'We're going to have the best time,' she murmurs. 'I've been waiting years for this, haven't you?'

Ohh, yes, I think dreamily. This feels so good, so right. There's almost no space between our faces. Bee's mouth tilts towards mine. She's going to taste warm and peppery, like summer roses.

My eyes fly open in revulsion. The whiff is so faint it's hardly there. But the spell is broken.

'Where did Tim go?' The question just bursts out.

Bee ripples like a mirage. For a terrifying moment I can see right through her. Then she goes back to normal. 'Pooh! Who cares about Supergeek?' she giggles. 'He is just a bad joke.'

Old and new memories rush at me. Two six-year-olds whispering under a table. An ancient book containing the forgotten rules of magic. A city where human souls are being traded for shadows.

Now the staticky odour in the DJ booth just makes me feel sick.

'This is pure fantasy,' I say loudly. 'What's happening in this city, that's real.'

My speech difficulty has gone as mysteriously as it came. There's a howl of feedback, and my amplified voice bounces back with added reverb.

'This is pure fantasy fantasy fantasy!'

The fans look puzzled, then the air fills with a new and chilling vibe. The lights go down until there's only a single harsh spotlight shining directly into my eyes.

'Loser!' someone yells.

The crowd takes up the insult, 'Loser! Loser! Loser!' hissing like snakes. I can't see their faces. They're dissolving like a dream, leaving me alone with something I now know for certain isn't Bee. I should be scared but I'm far too angry.

'Did you think I was that stupid?' I yell. 'Did you think you could *buy* me, with a DJ set and a gorgeous girl? Did you think I wouldn't notice that you stink of DEATH?'

Her eyes blaze with an inhuman light.

'Go to hell, Dino Skerakis!' she spits and slashes at my face.

I take a desperate step back and find myself falling through space.

CHAPTER 10

'YOU OK?'

Tim's voice is so close, I can feel his breath buzzing in my ear.

'Yeah. Yeah, I think so.'

I can barely make out his shape in the feeble light seeping down from above. We're back in the broken lift, still stuck between floors.

Physically I'm unharmed, but there's a familiar feeling of being smeared with some invisible evil residue. I drag myself into a sitting position. 'Jesus,' I groan. 'Serves me right.'

'Why, what happened?' Tim sounds panicky.

'Not sure,' I say quickly. 'Have you been waiting here all this time?'

He swallows. 'Dino, we just got here!'

'Are you serious? You didn't see that weird corridor?'

He sounds vague. 'A corridor? No. Is that what you saw?'

'Yeah,' I say. 'And what looked like offices. Not remotely supernatural; still, it's weird you don't remember.'

'Well, I don't,' he says in an edgy voice.

The light comes back on.

We blink like two stressed-out owls and the lift starts to move.

I imagine how I must have looked in the DJ booth, mouth hanging open with shock, while beautiful girls pleadingly reached out, calling my name. *The exact tunes.* It knew the exact tunes. It took everything I care about and made it seem cheap and stupid.

If Tim has no idea what happened, it's fine by me. Maybe one day I'll believe it never happened too.

My face is still burning as we walk out on to my floor. My mobile beeps.

Bee sounds frosty. 'Where the hell have you been?'

'It's complicated,' I hedge. 'I'll tell you when I see you.'

'Excellent,' she says in her new cold voice. 'Because I've just walked into your lobby.'

Our front door opens on a babble of voices. My cousin's family is leaving. 'Where'd you go?' Katinka says tragically. 'I *really* missed you.'

'Missed you too, Kittycat. I had to – I had to see someone.'

The lift comes clanking up the shaft and Bee gets out.

The next moments are surreal. My relatives pretending they haven't been analysing my weird behaviour in my absence. A very angry Bee registering what's happened to Mike and trying to disguise her shock.

I shepherd them down the corridor and shut us into the dump officially known as my bedroom.

Bee perches primly on my bed, like some visiting aunt.

Tim goes straight to the window and stares out. 'What's wrong with the fat guy?'

Bee gasps. 'You SAW that!'

I feel the room change shape.

'What the hell do you think is wrong, man?' I say carelessly. 'Mike's pushing forty and he's allergic to exercise. Plus all those boozy expense-account dinners –'

'Cut the crap!' Tim swings round. He's got this weird stretched look that makes the skin round his eyes look alarmingly transparent.

'You know what I'm talking about.' He sees my armchair and jerkily sits down. He covers his face. 'What the hell *was* that thing?'

I stop pretending I don't know what he's talking about.

'We don't know what the shadows are exactly,' I admit uncomfortably. 'We think it's what happens when people get too pally with our friend on the thirteenth floor. A kind of hole in, er, reality.'

I shoot a guilty glance at Bee. OK, so she's still mad with me for standing her up, but would it kill her to help me out here?

I hear Tim swallow. 'He has no idea, does he?'

'Mike? Not a clue.'

From what I know of Helen's husband, he probably regards a soul as some piece of nonessential software. All those months hanging round the Jobcentre had eaten away at his self-respect. Even I saw that. I guess he was so relieved at finding a way to get it back, he didn't think to check the small print. A soul for a shadow. A shadow for a soul.

Tim is back at the window, breathing hard.

'Know anything about biology?'

'Apart from the obvious smutty stuff, no,' I say, wondering where this is going. 'I quit the day they made us dissect those bull's eyes.'

Bee's silence is making me loathe the sound of my own voice.

'I'm in a fast-track biology class,' says Tim. 'Last

term we looked at cancer cells. You can't imagine the energy of those things. It's like they've been given some directive to take over the planet by Thursday. Growing and dividing, like some alien life form on fast forward. It's terrifying. At the same time they're – they're beautiful.'

'Beautiful?' I say incredulously.

Tim goes all crumpled and defeated. 'I knew you wouldn't understand.'

'No, really I do.'

It was easier when Tim Flowers was a joke. This kid is all nerve endings.

'Naturally you're freaked, man,' I say sympathetically. 'Those shadows freaked us the first time we went to the thirteenth floor. It's just, well, I hadn't exactly thought of them as beautiful.'

I see a flash of shock in Tim's eyes.

'You KNEW this might happen?'

'I didn't exactly –'

'You knew! And you still asked me to go up there!'

Bee goes pale. 'He did *what?*'

From their faces, you'd think *I* was the Lord of Lies himself.

Tim slides down the wall as if his legs have given

way. 'How can you fight that? How could you defend yourself against that kind of power?'

I'm burning with shame. I never gave a thought to the effect the thirteenth floor would have on Tim.

Despite his impressive new pecs, Tim is not a strong person. In my opinion the thirteenth floor let him off lightly, yet he's in bits. The haunted look in his eyes makes me long to turn the clock back.

I make encouraging noises. 'After your David batters the hell out of Goliath routine yesterday, I'd have said you'd defend yourself pretty well.'

'That was different,' he says bleakly. 'Those guys were human.'

'Erm,' says Bee in a weird voice. She's staring at my school bag.

Light rays are flooding out through the canvas, approximately where Marlon scribbled 'Marlon is the don!' in felt-tip.

Tim kneels down on the dusty carpet. 'What the hell have you got in there?' he says in an awed voice. 'Kryptonite?'

'Couldn't tell you,' I say too quickly.

He gasps. 'It couldn't be the book?'

I briefly imagine banging his head against the wall.

Bee goes dangerously still.

'He's kidding, right?' she says. 'You haven't really got the angel's book in your bag?'

'W-well, yeah –' I stammer. 'But –'

She almost stamps. 'I don't *believe* you, Dino! You found the book and you just didn't think to mention it!'

'I was going to, honestly,' I say miserably.

She's struggling to find words bad enough to describe me. 'You are really something else,' she gets out at last.

'I said I was going to tell you. It's blank anyway. You'd get more cosmic info in a cracker. It's not like a big deal!'

'It IS a big deal!' she blazes. 'I thought we were in this together. Apparently we're not.'

Tim gives us a beseeching look. 'Could you two fight later? This is amazing!'

Amazing doesn't begin to describe what's taking place. Like an overripe plum, the canvas of my bag is splitting open, carefully peeling away from its messy contents: a muddle of pens, rulers, gum wrappers, minidiscs, old tissues; and the book. Breaking all known laws of physics, a warm rosy light is streaming out from between its pages.

The crown of my head, my ribcage, the soles of my feet, grow hot and tingly with energy. This is not light. This is Light.

It flows purposefully through the room in a steady stream, subtly changing shape as it flows, though never into a shape I fully recognise.

Now and then it stops, examining my possessions with apparent interest. It doesn't really seem to be looking at, so much as *into*, things. Under its scrutiny, objects shimmer and turn transparent; a baseball cap, headphones, scuzzy old trainers, all become a see-through whirl of atoms.

It seems totally fascinated by my music magazines, fanning through pages like a bank teller. I hear Bee squeak as a series of well-known pop icons separate themselves from the glossy paper and briefly become three-dimensional. They hover like holographic messengers on a starship, making the room feel uncomfortably crowded, then silently sink back into the magazines. And still the light flows on.

When it reaches the heap of clothes beside my bed, it hesitates, as if it isn't sure how to proceed. A power surge lights up the room like a polaroid flash. To my embarrassment, the light morphs into four pairs of luminous hands and starts sorting briskly through my dirty laundry.

'What on *earth?*' I mutter.

The disembodied hands inspect each garment minutely, then send them winging towards the laundry basket.

Suddenly a familiar dayglo orange object falls out of a pocket in my jeans and goes spinning across the bare floorboards.

Tim makes a small strangled sound.

'No way,' breathes Bee.

The hands aren't just hands now, they're more like butterflies. Four sets of fingertips touch and close, hiding the toy from view.

The light grows so bright we have to shield our eyes.

They're taking out the evil vibes.

This thought could be mine, or it could be Tim's or Bee's. At this moment, I don't seem able to tell us apart.

I can't say how long this strange little ceremony goes on, because time doesn't seem to mean much. When the light withdraws at last, it's so gradual, there's no one moment when you could think, it's over.

It's a long time before we look at each other.

We're having to drag ourselves back from another

world. A world where it's feasible for a supernatural intelligence to hibernate inside a book for eight hundred years, come back to life, sort through your dirty laundry, and turn your entire world inside out and upside down.

I pick up the yo-yo. It feels lighter in a way I can't describe.

Tim and Bee both surreptitiously wipe their eyes.

Bee reaches out to touch the *Book of Light*. 'It feels warm,' she says in an awed voice. 'Can I?'

Her hand quivers as she opens the book. A breeze whispers into my room, bringing familiar flower scents, birdsong and flowing water.

She clutches me. 'Dino!'

A faint flush of colour has appeared in the margins of the book. The colours deepen as we watch; glittering gold and glowing crimson, intense emerald green and midnight blue. Swathes of foliage, saints, mythical birds and animals appear so smoothly on the creamy parchment, you'd think an invisible artist was painting them in front of our eyes.

'Turn the page!' I tell her urgently. 'Go *on*!'

I can't breathe. I'm going to see cosmic information that's been hidden for eight hundred years. Information which could help us defend ourselves against the darkness in this city.

The parchment crackles as Bee reverently turns the page.

But there are no words, not on the next page, nor any other.

'*Is* this meant to be like, a *joke*?'

I want to smash something, hit someone, anyone; I'm so mad with myself for believing.

'Dino, calm down!' Bee says. 'It's going to be OK! We're getting so close. We've just got to find a way to access the magic. I suppose they *had* to disguise it, to stop it falling into the wrong hands.'

'They?' I say blankly. 'Oh right, the angels!'

I'm sorry, I've strained my belief muscles to the max. I just can't relate to winged messengers wafting down from Heaven.

Bee suddenly registers that she's in the same room as Tim Flowers.

'Why are you here again?' she asks him in her princess voice.

'I invited him,' I say quickly.

'Even though you'd arranged to meet me?'

'I know, but then the book turned up in my locker,

and since neither of us knows Latin –'

Bee has a disbelieving glint in her eye. My lame excuse trails off.

'I had a few doubts,' I admit miserably. 'OK, a *lot* of doubts. Then Mike walked in and suddenly it was personal.'

'You didn't think my baby sister was personal?' she yells.

'It was for *you*! I'm talking about me. Then I saw Mike and I – I went totally mental, Bee. I needed someone to come to check out the thirteenth floor. Someone who –'

'– who wasn't a *girl*, perhaps?' Her tone is pure poison.

'It's got nothing to DO with that! Someone neutral. Someone who wasn't involved.'

We glare at each other, then Bee's expression softens.

'I suppose that makes a warped kind of sense.' She tentatively meets my eyes. 'It must have been horrible when you saw Mike.'

'Yeah, well, my boyhood hero and all that.'

Tim clears his throat. 'We should take the book to Mr Waverley.'

Bee looks appalled. 'Why, for Pete's sake?'

'It would be best,' says Tim stubbornly. 'He'll be at

the youth club now. It's only down the road.'

'No way,' says Bee. 'I'm not giving that creep the satisfaction.'

'You don't have to join his club,' I tell her. 'We're just asking for information. He obviously knows something, or why would he –'

'She couldn't join if she wanted to,' Tim interrupts earnestly. 'It's boys only. It's an old tra –' He claps his hand over his mouth as if he was on the verge of blurting out some big Boy's Annual secret.

Bee folds her arms. 'Oh, just *go*. Victor will be thrilled. Another bad boy saved from the streets.'

There's a tricky silence. Bee picks stonily at her fingernails.

Tim says nervously, 'Your dad – has *he* got a shadow?'

She spins. I genuinely think she's going to hit me. She almost spits, 'Did you tell Tim about my dad, Dino? Because that is just the lowest –'

'Bee, I *had* to! I had to make him see how –'

I stop trying to defend myself. I can go on telling myself I did it to get a result, but that isn't completely true and I know it.

It doesn't hurt to be nice, Dino. Well, I'm not. I'm not nice at all.

I hear Bee take a breath. 'The answer to your very personal question, Tim, is "I don't know". I haven't seen my dad since he told my mum about his creepy nocturnal deal. It's the kind of thing you'd rather not think about. I don't know if I could handle it.'

'I hope you never have to,' I say.

Bee gives me a wounded look. 'Well, you haven't exactly been Mr Reliable.' She goes back to picking her cuticles.

'Does that mean you're coming?' I ask hopefully.

She unexpectedly hooks her arm through Tim's. His face turns bright red.

'Come on,' she says in a tired voice. 'Take us to your leader!'

Dad hears us in the hall and peers round the sitting-room door.

'Later!' I call. 'Better be some of that cake left when I get back, you guys!'

The lift grinds and grates down to the ground floor. As I drag back the gates, I see the happy umbrella girl in the lobby. She doesn't seem nearly as happy as last time I saw her. 'Hey! It's my young Sir Galahad!' She's still smiling, but without her old sparkle.

I'm flattered she remembers but I can feel Bee

fidgeting, so I just say, 'Oh, hi. How's it all going?'

'I've been shopping. I've worn myself out.' She's wearing a midriff top which exposes her huge belly in a way I find extremely unnerving. Her T-shirt has a printed arrow pointing to the bulge and a cutesy message saying WORK IN PROGRESS.

Bee suddenly steps forward. 'Hi, Sadie.'

The girl's face lights up. 'Angel! You came to see me!'

Bee gestures vaguely. 'Actually, I really came to –'

Sadie's eyes grow round 'This is your boyfriend? I had no idea!'

'We're really just friends,' I say hastily.

My head is spinning. The happy umbrella girl is Jimmie Molloy's girlfriend. That terrifying swelling is their unborn child, Bee's baby sister.

Sadie impulsively seizes Bee's hands. 'Can't I persuade you to come up? I bought the cutest baby dungarees. They've got teeny hollyhocks on the hems. I'm desperate to show somebody. I could show your father, when he comes back, but you know what men are like!'

Bee looks bewildered. 'Comes back? Where'd he go?'

'Oh, some work thing. It was rather last minute.'

'But Dad always tells me if he's going away.' Bee sounds about six years old.

'I'm sure he would have, sweetie,' Sadie says. 'But some big business crisis came up, you know how it is.'

Bee frowns. 'Yeah, I guess.'

Sadie doesn't seem to notice Bee is surreptitiously trying to free herself. 'I told him, "Jimmie, you have the worst timing!" I mean, this little one's due any minute!' She goes into peals of nervous laughter. 'Just hope she doesn't pop out on Halloween! Who *knows* what'd come out!'

She's trying to joke, but her eyes have a pleading expression. 'So will you keep me company for an hour? We could order takeaway from the Yellow River?'

'I really have to –'

'This place is so quiet. Sometimes I think – oh, well, I guess all new mums get into silly panics, don't they?'

My stomach churning. She knows. Sadie knows her baby is in danger.

Bee gives me a trapped look. 'We were going out. I suppose it could wait.'

'Yeah,' I say. 'It can wait.'

Sadie almost bursts into tears. 'Angel, thank you!'

'We'll keep you posted,' I tell Bee.

'You'd better.'

I see her straighten her shoulders as she follows her father's girlfriend into the lift. 'So what else have you been buying for that little designer sprog you've got in there?' she asks. 'Have you got into Osh Kosh Begosh yet? They do really cool stuff.' The cage judders out of sight and Bee's bright voice fades into the distance.

Tim looks distressed. 'He's run out on her, hasn't he? They always say it's business. They say, "I hate leaving you, but I have to go where the money is."'

'Who says that?'

He's staring down at his shoes. 'My dad. Oh well.' He gives a ghost of a shrug. 'Don't suppose I'm the son of his dreams.'

'But your mum's all right?' I say quickly. 'You're probably tight with your mum?'

Too late, I remember the rumours about him living with his gran.

I can see he's trying to figure out an explanation that won't blow up in our faces and upset us both.

'I'm afraid my mum's not actually around any more,' he says carefully in his Supergeek voice. 'My dad has had to face a number of disappointments in his life.'

If I could I'd get Tim Flowers reincarnated with a new set of parents. Instead, I fall back on the thing guys do when things get too painful. I give him a friendly male thump. 'You'll be OK, man. You're a powerful Jedi now!'

He looks panic-stricken. 'What made you say that?'

'Well – you do all that cool karate.'

'Oh, right!'

His relief is audible, almost like he was scared he'd given something away.

'You knew about the book, didn't you?' I ask abruptly. 'When I showed it to you, you knew exactly what it was.'

Tim glances at his watch. 'We should go. Mr Waverley hates it if we're late.'

I'm almost sure he's avoiding my question but I give him the benefit of the doubt.

'Take a deep breath,' I warn. 'It's going to be weird out there.'

It's grown foggy since I walked home from school. People emerge and disappear from swirls of vapour like ghosts. We almost collide with a young woman hurrying along with a baby buggy.

In the street light, Tim's face is suddenly the colour of old cheese.

'Her eyes!' he says shakily. 'Did you see her eyes? They look –'

It's not just the shadows or the fog. It's a disturbingly familiar feeling that I seem to recognise from my new, extremely tiring dreams. A sense of not quite seeing, or, worse, almost glimpsing something, just as it melts back into the dark . . .

A harassed father trudges past, carrying a giant pizza box in one hand and a bag of groceries in the other. One of his kids is whingeing pathetically because it can't keep up.

'Did you feel it?' Tim says in a scared voice.

'Yeah, yeah, I feel it,' I say. 'You don't have to look at them all.'

He's still staring with a sick fascination.

'It pulls. It's like – like a tide pulling at you.' I drag him away but he keeps looking back. 'It can tune into our thoughts, did you know that?'

'Yeah, I know,' I say. 'But –'

There's a new edge in his voice. 'Dino, it knows everything we think.'

'It's a nightmare, mate. But you mustn't –'

'You don't know me!' he says angrily. 'You don't have the first idea what goes on in my head when I turn out the light.'

I'm going to crack some dirty joke to bring him back

192

down to earth, but suddenly he's clutching at my sleeve. I see pure terror in his eyes.

'Did you ever want something really badly?' he croaks.

'For real. Plenty of things –' I start.

'Not like that,' he says desperately. 'Not stupid trainers or getting picked for some moronic team. I mean so, so badly, you'd – you'd crawl down almost any hole to get it?' His face twists. It's like he's arguing with someone I can't see.

'I don't think I have,' I say.

He sags like an old man. 'Course not,' he says in a defeated voice. 'Dino Skerakis wouldn't have to.'

I try my best to sound flip and normal. 'They say everyone's got a price,' I tell him. 'You have to hope you'd have the guts to say no. You have to hope you're bigger than that.'

Somehow I've hit the right upbeat tone. By the time we reach the converted church which doubles as an inner-city community centre, he's almost back to his old Supergeek self.

'There's been a church on this spot since the Middle Ages,' he says pompously. 'Maybe you didn't know that, Dino?'

'I don't think I did, Tim,' I say. 'Thank you for telling me.'

Tim's face gets that taut look, like pastry rolled too thin. 'I can't help how I talk!' He checks himself. 'What's the use?' he mutters miserably.

He points out the cubby hole in the corridor where Victor has his office, then dashes off to get changed. Through the open door, I can see Victor Waverley perched casually on his desk, settling some dispute between two little thugs.

One has self-inflicted tattoos on his knuckles, the ones that say LOVE and HATE. His shaved head, together with having no neck, makes him looks like a baby pit bull. The other kid wears a massive padded jacket and some kind of flying helmet, probably the last word in street cool if you're twelve.

I wait until Waverley registers me standing there.

He whips off his specs as if he thinks he's hallu-cinating. 'We'll sort it out later,' he tells the boys.

Without glasses, he looks like a different person: tougher, more complicated.

He pulls out a chair. 'Dino, isn't it? To what do I owe this, erm, pleasure?'

I get straight to the point. 'I've got the book.'

Waverley looks blank. 'Sorry? Not with you.'

'The one James Wilkins talks about. The one that disappeared?'

Feeling flustered, I try again.

'The one that was dictated to Amb –'

He raises his hand like a traffic cop. 'Hold up. I'm confused. The boy who says there is no magic land at the top of the Faraway Tree wants me to believe he has acquired a book dictated by an *angel*?'

Does he have to talk so loud? I feel my face start to burn.

'I know what I said. But that was before.'

'Before –?'

'Before I – before I went to the thirteenth floor and realised some of this stuff was actually true.'

He interrupts again. 'Let me get this straight. Not only have you acquired a long-lost angelic manuscript, you also had a sneaky peek at our local Twilight Zone? Were you by any chance captured by alien beings while you were there and subjected to unpleasant anatomical probings?'

'No, and I didn't see Elvis or his freaking blue suede shoes,' I say angrily. 'But I went and I can prove it.'

He frowns and leans back in his chair. 'I'm listening.'

'I found that dead kid's yo-yo. Actually it kind of threw itself at me and attached itself to my finger. Bee and I were totally creeped out by the whole experience.'

'You went together? Why did you do that?'

I don't want to discuss Bee's private business with her mother's boyfriend, plus I can't quite bring myself to mention supernatural shadows to an adult authority figure, so I fudge a little.

'Yeah, we decided to check it out. Your lesson got us all intrigued.'

'Is that so?'

'Totally. We wanted to see if it had any basis in fact.' I give him a quick glance to see how this is going down. 'Guess we got more than we bargained for.'

Waverley's eyes don't leave my face. 'Go on.'

'We were both creeped out, like I said. We wanted some answers. Bee said we should read that old local history book you gave me, *A Mystic's Whatever*. We read the whole thing, then Bee – this will probably sound unbelievable – she said we should look for the lost manuscript, and next thing it just turns up in my locker.'

'As you say, it sounds totally unbelievable.'

Waverley's voice is detached, almost cold.

'It was blank when I first got it,' I explain. 'Then it changed.'

I start to unzip my jacket.

'Not here!' he says quickly. 'Just describe how it changed.'

'It was like – you know those kids' magic painting books, where you just brush on water? Beautiful little medieval pictures just came up out of the parchment like they'd been there all the time. And they've got this like, *glow*, like coloured glass when the sun shines through. It – well, it blew us away.'

'I'm assuming it took more than tap water to trigger this transformation?' Waverley's voice suddenly has an edge.

I shake my head. 'I have NO idea. I'd just come back from my trip to the thirteenth floor. The second trip, that is. And I was pretty freaked –'

'You went BACK?'

'I was worried I was going schizo or something.' I find myself having to swallow. 'I was seeing things I couldn't rationally explain –'

'Did you go back alone or with Bee?'

'Does it matter who I went with? The thing is, when I got back, this light –'

'It matters,' Waverley says harshly. 'I need to know, as a matter of urgency, if you went alone or if someone went with you?'

'He went with me,' says a scared voice.

Tim appears beside me. His face is scarlet.

Waverley whips off his specs. '*What?*'

'He went with me,' Tim mumbles. 'Dino needed me to help him check something out.'

In one furious movement, Waverley sweeps everything off his desk. Files, pens, a mug filled with cold tea go crashing to the ground.

'How could you be so STUPID?'

'Hey, man, don't take it out on him,' I say uncomfortably. 'He didn't want to come, but I put on the pressure, OK?'

It's the first time I've seen Victor Waverley lose his temper. It isn't just anger I hear in his voice. It's despair. 'What you both did was nothing short of lunacy. Tim, you've been training for less than a year. Heaven knows what damage you've done to yourself – and to the Work.'

That's how he says it. The Work.

The ruckus has attracted attention. Boys are appearing from everywhere. Some are really young, eight or nine at most. I recognise three of the older boys from Urban Legends. A few are wearing proper martial arts gear. Most wear street clothes that say, *Back off! I'm hard.*

The pit bull kid rushes in. 'What's going on?'

Waverley gets himself under control. 'I'm going to break one of our rules,' he tells the boys. 'We'll have to take Dino down to the basement.'

The boys nod expressionlessly, as if the word 'basement' has some weird significance.

I'm getting an unpleasant feeling in the back of my neck. I start to back towards the door. 'I should go.'

Three boys silently position themselves in front of the exit.

'I'm not happy about this, Dino,' Waverley says in a regretful voice. 'But actions have consequences, you see.'

The boys do another round of synchronised nodding. Except for Tim, who looks as if he'd like to crawl under a stone.

'You can't keep me here!'

I feel as if I'm free-falling into Looking-glass World. Waverley unlocks a drawer and takes out a large old-fashioned key. Before I realise what's happening, I'm being marched through the community centre. We come to an ancient oak door so riddled with woodworm it looks like a massive wooden honeycomb.

Waverley fits the key in, and the door opens, exhaling a dank smell of earth and cellars. Waverley shepherds me ahead of him down a flight of stone steps. The only light is what seeps down from upstairs.

At the bottom is another door. This time the security arrangements are strictly twenty-first century. Waverley taps in a code and the door clicks open. I stumble ahead of him into the dark. My palms are clammy with fear. What the hell has Waverley got down here? The corpse of every kid who ever crossed him in class?

There's a crisp scratch as Waverley strikes a match. He lights a storm lantern and holds it up so I can see my surroundings.

Run, Dino! I think.

I'm in a perfectly circular room. The floor tiles are painted with unmistakably magical symbols. In the centre is what looks like the jagged remains of an ancient oak tree.

I can hear the drip and bubble of water. The boys file silently to a shadowy recess. I catch glints of metal in the lantern-light, as they lift down bizarre old relics which belong in a museum: helmets of beaten metal, chain-mail tunics. With smooth synchronised movements, they put them on.

It's like they're growing up in front of my eyes. The antiquated garb instantly turns the kids into tough, if short, medieval men.

'I'm happy for you guys!' I say. 'It must be nice coming down here to stage your little re-enactments or whatever. But like I say, I should go.'

The door closes behind me with a dull *thunk*.

Waverley moves the lantern, letting the thin wash of light track across a crude stone wall glittering with weapons: ancient battleaxes, spears, longbows and swords.

I feel a spurt of fear. It's not a re-enactment. It's a cult. A mad homicidal medieval cult. Waverley has brainwashed these misfits into mindless obedience. I can tell because they've got the weirdly calm expressions brainwashed people have in movies. Like Tim! That's exactly how he looked when he took on that gang.

My heart is thumping so hard, I feel as if I'm going to suffocate, but I'm frantically trying not to let it show.

'Here's something that might interest you.'

Waverley shines the light into an alcove, illuminating a list of names carved in the stone.

The name at the top of the list sends shock waves into my belly.

Will Burbage. The outlaw-turned-monk, who carried out Ambrose's dying wish. Towards the bottom, a second name jumps out. James Wilkins – author of *A Mystic's Life*.

Waverley takes off his glasses. 'I'm really just the latest in a long line.'

What he's trying to tell me is so outrageous that my mind refuses to take it in.

Victor Waverley smiles for the first time. 'Tell him, Kyle.'

The pit bull kid folds his arms. 'He's the Guardian, fool. He's come to save the city.'

CHAPTER 11

EXCEPT for the faint hissing from the lamp, the room is silent. Waverley and the boys are watching me, waiting for me to react.

'Nah, I don't buy that,' I say dismissively. 'That's a story for little kids. Anyway, the Guardian was always holed up in some secret hide-out.'

'There's more than one way of hiding,' Waverley says softly. 'Showing up in a way people don't expect works almost as well.'

He deliberately meets my eyes.

I'm all set to make some smart crack, but something in his face brings me up short.

'So where are the warriors?' I bluster. 'Aren't you supposed to be training your hotshot warriors for the final showdown?'

Kyle gives a deeply irritated sigh.

The other boys struggle to keep straight faces.

'I can understand this isn't exactly how you

imagined us.' Waverley sounds oddly sympathetic.

I'm having that eerie feeling I had in the internet café. The universe of space and time is unravelling around me. And suddenly I know.

I know why Tim acted so freaked when I made my Jedi crack. He thought I'd blown Waverley's cover. This is no inner-city boys' club. It's an underground army. A secret army of twenty-first-century knights!

Victor Waverley lifts something from a shelf, a well-worn wooden goblet that must have been handed down from medieval times. A shiver goes down my back as I realise where the sounds of bubbling water are coming from. Waverley leans into the hollow tree stump, dips in the goblet and gives it to me, brimming.

I don't happen to like drinking out of an old wooden cup that has been touched by however many unwashed mouths, but I shut my eyes and drink the teeth-achingly cold water from Ambrose's well. And in that moment I understand something for the first time.

It isn't over.

The trees, wolves and medieval charcoal burners might be gone. And maybe earth and heaven are no longer so intimately connected as they were then. But the unknown unknowable forces which turned

Ambrose's life inside out are still rippling through our lives.

I wipe my mouth, give the goblet back to Waverley, and draw a deep, very frightened breath.

'Tell me what I have to do.'

I learn a lot in Waverley's martial arts class. How to block my opponent's move. How to use his own life-force against him. But mostly what I learn is how to fall flat on my backside, get up with reasonable good humour, and try again.

At the end of the session I'm aching all over. Victor Waverley gives the impression he could keep going all night. I don't know where that guy learned his particular fighting style, but he makes Tim's performance at Legends look like child's play.

When he asks me to stay behind after the class, I'm secretly thrilled. Finally the confusing events of the last few days are going to be be explained. Then Waverley, aka the Light Guardian of Tina's legends, will tell me how to make everything right again.

I've seen Waverley handle a hall full of kids who'd normally be headed straight for juvenile court, and I know, without a doubt, that he's who he says he is.

Down here, he emanates an authority you can't ignore.

I follow him into the community centre's tiny kitchen. Waverley unlocks a cupboard, finds clean mugs and tea bags, and asks if I take sugar. To get the milk out of the fridge, he has to take off the padlock.

When Tina told us the stories about the Guardian, I pictured him hiding out in a honeycomb of secret caves under the city, sleeping on animal skins, cooking over wood fires. I certainly didn't imagine him in this tacky kitchen fossicking with padlocks and making tea.

'Bee says when I was a little kid I told her I used to know the rules of magic,' I say in a hinting voice. 'She says it's like I *knew* about Ambrose's book even then.'

I'm hoping this will be the start of the deeply satisfying conversation where I finally find out what part I play in the cosmic showdown that's been coming for almost a thousand years.

Waverley hands me my tea. 'We'll probably be more comfortable in my office.'

I trail after him like a puppy and try again. 'So how do you plan to take out this thing on the thirteenth floor?'

He sighs, and I can tell he's trying to be patient. 'I'd have thought that by this time you'd have figured out that this "thing" is not something anyone can just "take out".'

I'm confused. 'So why are you training all these warriors?'

'They're not warriors, not in the way you mean. These boys are sent to me for a variety of reasons. I try to teach them to become strong, disciplined individuals.'

'By getting them to dress up in chain mail!'

'By teaching them how to protect themselves from the illusions emanating from the thirteenth floor. Whatever your legends might say, I am not grooming an elite fighting force.'

'Are you sure your boys understand the distinction?' I ask huffily. 'Tim for instance? Because the other night he sure as hell looked like he was fighting to me.'

Waverley ignores the dig. 'I train them to the best of my, and their, ability. Twice a week they come down here and I show them every technique I know, to help them survive an encounter with the dark entity that has set up shop in our city.' He shoots me a meaningful look. 'And it's not enough.'

I feel a thrill of excitement. Now we're getting to it. I decide to help him out. 'There's one thing I don't understand. If this book is so sacred, how come you entrusted it to me?'

Waverley gives an exasperated groan. 'Dino, this is not TV. You were not "chosen" for an heroic task.'

I'm still raw from my humiliation on the thirteenth floor, and I don't appreciate being patronised. I scowl at him. 'You were chosen, weren't you?'

'How I became a Guardian is none of your business. We were talking about you. You were not chosen. You and Bee jumped in with your flat feet, making an unstable cosmic situation ten times more dangerous. Which at this time of year was downright reckless.'

'Oh, I get it!' I pull a spooky face. 'Because it's Halloween!'

Waverley makes an exasperated noise. 'You kids will swallow any kind of garbage, won't you, if it flatters your egos? You're even willing to believe you're a superhero in disguise. But you refuse to take *anything* seriously. Yes, Dino! Because it's Halloween, the time when . . .'

'Skip the lecture, OK?' I say angrily. 'Do me a favour and assume I already know about Halloween, and stick to the freaking point. If I'm not the chosen whoever, why give me your precious book?'

'I'm in agreement with you, Dino,' he says coolly.

'Let's stick to the point. Point one. You and Bee blundered on to the thirteenth floor like a pair of suicidal babes in the wood. Point two. I strongly doubted that either of you had the experience to handle the repercussions by yourselves.' Waverley gives me his sideways grin. 'Unfortunately, you both distrusted, not to say actively disliked me.'

I start to mumble something.

'Don't apologise! It was an added complication, that's all. Taking other factors into account, I took a calculated risk, and trusted that the book would lead you to us and to the work.'

'So you're saying me being involved is just like, an accident?'

'I'm saying you made a choice. Now you're dealing with consequences, as I said before.'

No destiny, no patterns of hidden meaning, just the busy human brain spinning stories out of dross.

'Then why bother to come to our school and get everyone hot and bothered about the legends?' I can hear my voice cracking with self-pity.

Victor Waverley sighs and takes off his glasses.

'I wanted – I wanted you all to wake up before it was too late.'

'Will you stop talking in riddles! Wake up to *what*?'

'To reality, Dino. To reality.'

He's using his street voice now. I thought he was putting it on when he first came to our school. But this is really who he is. I feel ashamed. Waverley's trying to be straight with me and I'm acting like a brat.

'Don't you get it?' he says. 'This isn't about *you*, man. It isn't about being special. It's so much bigger than you or me. If you can't understand anything else, can you at least try to understand that?'

No one ever talked to me like this before. I don't know what I'm meant to say. To hide my confusion, I take a sip of tea, and choke. It's the most revolting fluid I have ever tasted in my life.

Waverley pulls a face. 'I've been told I should stick to coffee.'

'Man, you should market it as pesticide! This is *rough*!' I push the cup away. 'So is Halloween a good time to, you know, vanquish the –?'

'It's the only time, fool,' he says. 'Think about it. The angelic material inside the book has been reactivated. But the rules of magic, as you call them, haven't yet revealed themselves.'

'I don't underst –'

'Think of the book as a blank cheque for infinite cosmic power. Now add Halloween to the mix.'

I shake my head. 'Still don't get it.'

'You do know how Halloween got to be such a big deal?'

'Oh, now, let me see,' I say. 'Earth turning away from the sun. Shorter days. Long dark nights. Oh, no! What's that flitting through the graveyard? Could it be that the veil between the worlds is growing thin?' I give a scornful laugh. 'Then humans discovered electricity and it all seemed a bit silly.'

Waverley shakes his head. 'Not really. The discovery of electricity just lulled people into a false sense of security. We forgot that the waning of the light occurs on more than a physical level.'

I find myself remembering the blissful atmosphere in my room when Light, with a capital L, started pouring from my school bag. But I don't know how to talk about that, so I say, 'Light *is* physical. You see it or you don't.'

'You think? You walked here tonight. You must have noticed something? Or did Dino Skerakis just turn up his collar and tell himself it was unusually foggy out?'

I shift uncomfortably. I've been trying to forget

about our walk. 'No, it feels weird out there,' I say in a low voice.

'It's like water lilies,' says Waverley. 'First there's one or two floating on the surface of the pond. Days pass. One or two more appear, and maybe just one or two more. Then one night something tips the balance. Next morning the entire pond is so choked with flowers, all the fish are floating, belly up, from lack of oxygen.'

I feel something cold creep up my spine. I absolutely know Waverley isn't talking about lilies.

'There used to be a general agreement that reality was solid and measurable,' he says. 'Time. Space. What goes up must come down. Now it seems increasingly as if reality is something we're all creating together. Unfortunately, this only works if everyone is awake.'

It's like he's using code he hopes I'll figure out later.

'This is decision time,' he says. 'You don't have to be a Guardian to know that. Stick your head out of any window in this town and you'll smell it in the air. The question is, do we want to survive?'

I swallow.

'If we do, we'd better wake up damn quick and start creating a new and better reality. Our enemy knows that. He knew his time would come. That's why he's been working twenty-four-seven to get us into his power, picking us off over the centuries; one by one, soul by soul by soul. Slow work. Very slow.'

Waverley takes off his glasses. He rubs his eyes. For the first time he looks bone-tired.

'He knows how it works, you see. He's calculating that some day soon, tomorrow or the next day, if we're really unlucky, it could even be tonight, that balance is going to tip in his direction.'

I feel an ache inside which doesn't seem to be entirely mine.

'What will happen?' I ask huskily, 'if the balance, you know –?'

'Sure you want to know?' He takes a breath. 'Basically, he gets to say what's real.'

The building goes so silent, I can hear it roaring in my ears. No traffic, no sudden life-giving blast of hip hop or banghra. No yelling in the street. Then there's a click and a heavy whirr as the refrigerator turns itself on further down the hall.

'I'm not saying this to scare you,' Waverley says, 'but the *Book of Light* is probably more vulnerable than at any time in its history.'

I try to smile. 'It's lucky I brought it back to you, before all the Halloween creepies come out of the woodwork.'

He shakes his head. 'You and Bee are the book's keepers now.'

My jaw drops. 'But you said –'

'We're fairly sure the *Book of Light* was fitted with some kind of angelic timelock after Ambrose died.'

'A timelock?'

'It's a logical deduction. A book transcribed and bound by humans, that then became mysteriously inaccessible to humans. Until now.'

I stare at him. 'Me and Bee *activated* it?'

'It certainly looks that way. I don't understand it, and I deeply regret it, but I'd be stupid to ignore it. As a Guardian you learn to trust these things.'

I blow out my breath. 'We screwed up, didn't we?'

'You had insufficient information. No one can blame you for that.'

Waverley claps me on the shoulder. 'Go home, man, and have a hot bath, or your muscles will hurt like hell in the morning.'

I walk back home in a daze. I keep peeling off layers but, instead of answers, I only find a deeper darker mystery.

In the sitting room the only light is from the TV. Film footage of some terrorist outrage flickers silently across the screen. Dad is snoozing peacefully. I clear my throat and he wakes with a start. For an instant he looks baffled, then he beams. 'You're home!'

'Mum gone to bed?'

'I packed her off.' He yawns and stretches. 'Want a snack?'

'Are you offering?'

'You think I want you dropping your sordid tomato ketchup all over my work surfaces? Yes, my beautiful mutant boy! I'm offering!'

I perch on a stool in the kitchen and Dad sets out titbits on the counter: hunks of bread, olives, crumbly cubes of feta, a saucer of mind-blowing garlicky dip.

'The girls are going to love me tomorrow!' I tell him.

Dad gives me a sly smile. 'What do you think makes Greek men so virile?'

'Ooh, this is a long shot, but I'm guessing – erm, garlic?'

We chat about neutral father–son topics: football, the worrying new sound in the car that might be a slipping fanbelt; and while we talk, Dad beats eggs, dices onions and courgette, and tears fresh coriander leaves off the pot plant on the windowsill.

'Dad, that stuff smells like tomcats!' I complain.

'On its own. But with the eggs, it's *thavmaseo!*'

Dad hardly ever talks Greek these days but, for the bizarre yet strangely delicious chemistry of eggs with coriander, only his mother tongue will do.

Some fathers would give their son a hard time for acting the way I did this morning; mine just feeds me and calls me his beautiful boy.

I've got into a habit of treating my old man like some comical old dinosaur whose day is basically done. He *is* a dinosaur in a lot of ways. His taste in music, to name one. And he's got this major bee in his bonnet about honesty.

'I don't *care* if the company is covered by insurance,' he bellowed, when I'd been offered some totally untraceable sound equipment. 'I don't *care* if everybody does it. I will NOT have stolen goods in this house!'

But tonight I see my father in a new light. I see how his old sweater is having to stretch across his soft podgy belly, and how the odd wiry white hair has started to sprout among his eyebrows, as well as the tufts in his hair, and suddenly I want to stop time in its tracks. I want to beg my dad, 'Don't ever change.'

'I'm bushed,' I mumble. 'Better go and crash.'

Dad gives me one of his bone-crushing hugs. I feel a new exhaustion emanating from him, an odour almost.

'You're a good boy,' he murmurs. 'I know things haven't been – I know things haven't –'

He can't seem to complete the sentence. He looks bewildered. I have a sudden chilling sense that he isn't quite sure where he is. I put my hand on his arm. 'Dad? Are you OK?'

A split second later he's back behind his eyes. He looks shaken, but he tries to laugh it off. 'I'm fine. Your old man just needs to get his head down. It's been a long day.'

He insists he's OK, so I go off to my room. I hear Mum's anxious voice and Dad grumbling. 'Fuss fuss. You women drive me crazy.'

After the usual plumbing noises, the flat goes quiet.

I almost doze off, then pure panic sends me bolt upright.

I scrabble around in the dark until I find the angel's book. I place the miraculous manuscript under my pillow, pull the covers over my head and drop into a dreamless sleep.

* * *

Minutes later, it seems, bright sunlight is glittering on my eyelashes.

Crap, I've overslept! It's dark lately when my alarm goes off. Why didn't someone wake me? I grope for the clock on my bedside table. It isn't there. Nor is the table.

That's because this isn't actually my room. There are glowstars on the ceiling. The shelves are crammed with teddy bears and Barbie dolls, plus the usual tasteless Barbie accessories. It's a little girl's room, by the look of it, from the days before PlayStations and Furbies.

A small child is curled up on the pink-and-white bed, fast asleep on top of the covers. She looks the age you'd expect the owner of this bedroom to be, around six or seven years old; a rather severe little girl actually. A wide gold streak gleams among her dark curls. Her skin is the colour of very lightly toasted almonds.

As I stare in bewilderment, Bee's child self morphs gently into Bee as she is now, in a white midriff T-shirt and jeans.

I have *no* idea what's going on, but I'd better get out before Bee wakes up and finds me lurking in her bedroom. I've barely formed this thought when she stirs drowsily.

218

She sits up with a gasp. 'Where on earth –?'

'Bee, I swear, this was a big surprise to me too. I just woke up and – Jesus!'

There's a sharp tingling sensation, not unlike being dragged through a nettle patch, and Bee walks right through me and out of the door.

Oh my God, I'm a ghost! My heart just stopped in my sleep, like those horrifying obituaries Aunt Tippie reads out to my mum of apparently strapping healthy sports-playing teenage boys who were actually just living on borrowed time.

Now my disembodied spirit is flitting about in, what do they call that clearing-house-type place between the worlds? Limbo? Or is limbo something else? Either way, the thought of living out my days as a ghost is totally unhinging. I go tearing after Bee in a panic. She hasn't gone far. She's at the top of the stairs, gazing around, totally bewildered.

'This is like our old house,' she murmurs. 'But it's so bright. I don't remember it being so bright.'

Thick golden light is pouring through doors and windows, making it seem as if the whole house is swimming in honey.

Bee half floats downstairs through the golden haze.

'Careful!' I yell. 'Something very weird is going on.'

The good news is, I'm almost certain I'm not dead. I think it's a dream; I just don't know whose.

Voices drift from an open door. I hear a familiar laugh.

'Jimmie, you're crazy,' someone says affectionately.

Bee's face fills with naked longing.

'I don't believe it,' she whispers. 'This isn't happening.'

I follow her across the light-drenched hall. I can smell woodsmoke.

Bee's parents are in the living room, in front of a crackling open fire. Cuddling on the sofa, in stone-washed jeans and T-shirts, they could be posing for a celebrity photo-shoot. They have that super-real airbrushed shimmer.

Claudette Molloy smiles at her daughter. 'We were coming to look for you!'

Bee is dazed. 'You were?'

'Tell her the news, Jimmie,' her mum says.

'She knows!' chuckles Bee's dad. 'Look at her face.'

'Do you, darling? Have you guessed why Daddy's here?' Claudette sounds like a breathless little girl.

Bee stands completely still. She's afraid to move or even breathe in case this beautiful bubble bursts and she finds herself back in William Blake Crescent with one parent instead of two. This is what she wants. Everyone together, all happy and shimmery. She wants it so badly I can feel it, like toothache.

'You two made up?' she says in a small voice. 'I mean, *really*?'

'We really made up.' Her dad pats the sofa. 'Sit down, princess.'

'Daddy just landed a wonderful job,' her mum coos. 'That's how we managed to buy our old house back.'

And I'm Priscilla Queen of the Desert.

'And Sadie? And her baby?' I call out to Bee. 'Where do they fit in?'

I've figured out whose dream I'm in and I feel terrible. Any minute now Jimmie Molloy is going to swear he's a reformed character.

'I know you've heard it before,' he says on cue. 'But I've totally changed. I haven't had a drink for weeks. And I've given up gambling. There's only room in my life for one addiction, from now on. My family. You, your mother and me. That's all I want. It's all I've ever wanted.' He takes his daughter's hands. 'The bad times are over. You don't have to be brave any more.'

Bee's shoulders start to quiver. She just sits

there shaking, making absolutely no sound. It's like there's this storm of feelings inside her but she can't let it out.

Her father seems upset. 'I thought you'd be happy.'

Bee makes a sound that could be a sob or a gasp of pain. 'Happy?' she says in a choked voice. 'I've been dreaming of this ever since I was seven! I just can't believe –'

'Believe,' he says softly. 'Because it's true. Your mother is the only woman for me, Bee. I see that now. I've come to my senses.'

He tilts her chin, and she dares to meet his eyes. Her face is trembling and her eyes are shining with so much love, I have to clench my fists.

Still shaking with emotion, Bee goes to throw her arms around him.

She pulls back. Her nostrils flare with disgust.

'Who are you people? Who are you really?'

'Bee, please don't let's have a drama,' says her mother.

Bee jumps up, backing away from the people on the sofa.

'I said, who ARE you?'

'Calm down!' says Bee's father. 'There's no call for this.'

'You spoil everything,' her mum complains. 'I've finally got a chance to be happy, but you're ruining it just like you always do.'

Bee literally changes colour. This is so close to her own secret fear, she almost believes it's her real-life mother, spitting poison.

Then she does this amazing thing. Bee wakes up inside her dream. I see it in her eyes, like a light coming on.

'This is pure lies,' she says wonderingly. She turns on them in a sudden fury. 'My real mother would never try to blackmail me like that. And you're nothing like my father. You're old and cold and you smell like – like a rotting corpse!'

Whoosh! The fireplace becomes a raging furnace. Flames shoot out of power sockets. In that terrifying chain reaction you get in dreams, rugs and upholstery instantly set themselves ablaze. The air swims with supernatural heat.

Bee's fake parents continue to sit on the burning sofa, like giant puppets. I watch them melt slowly first through the charred suede, trickling down through coiled springs and horsehair, in rivulets like molten candle wax and finally vanishing between the floorboards.

223

CRASH! Windows burst in, exploding tiny glass fragments everywhere. Chunks of ceiling come smashing down. And something dark and vengeful comes swirling through the wreckage.

'Bee – look out!' I scream.

She spins and sees me through the inferno. '*Dino?*'

Something's bleeping. The daylight coming through my window is very nearly as weak as Aunt Tippie's tea, but it's genuine daylight.

I roll over and switch off my alarm.

I'm in bed, in my own room. It's morning in the real world.

Did that just happen? Could two people be so closely connected they can share the same dream?

I turn cold. What if it was just a ruse to keep me distracted?

The book! I make a lunge for my pillow.

At that moment Mum pops her head round my door. She's got her coat on.

'Just checking you didn't sleep through your alarm.'

'Hi! No, actually, amazingly I didn't!'

I must look like a bad statue, Guilty Boy in Boxers, fake grin, fingers unnaturally splayed on my pillows. Are my pillows normally this bulky? I can't tell. I can't feel if it's still there.

'So are you off to work now?' I hint hopefully.

'Decided I deserved a day off,' she says. 'I went to buy your dad a paper. He's determined this is the last week he's helping Uncle Nicky at Zorba's.'

Mum is her usual upbeat self yet I get the feeling she's inwardly bracing herself for some new ordeal. She's probably worrying how we'll live on her wages, if Dad doesn't manage to find a proper job.

'Mum, did you come in for a reason? Because I've really got to –'

'No reason!' she says quickly. 'Just checking my handsome son is still alive. Think you could get home early tonight, petal? I'll get your dad to cook something nice.'

'Mum, I'll try but I honestly can't promise. We've got this big match coming up. Our coach says –'

She vanishes in a heartbeat. Any mention of sport and my mother switches off. I let go my breath, but next minute she's back.

'Careful when you go out,' she says anxiously. 'It's so foggy, you wouldn't see the car until it knocked you down.'

I'm sweating by this time. What am I, some brainless warthog? I had no business going to sleep. I'm its keeper. It was my freaking *duty* to stay up. When I'm sure she's gone, I throw the pillows aside, and almost burst into tears. The book is still there.

I touch it softly and feel that faint mysterious springtime vibe.

Suddenly I don't care that I have no idea how to make the *Book of Light* unlock its secrets. I can't see my own DNA, or radio waves. It doesn't mean they're not there. In a weird way, not knowing makes the book more precious. Maybe I'm not chosen, or in any way special, but for the time being I'm the book's keeper, and I'm going to put it in the safest place I can think of.

I drag a suitcase out from under my bed, bury the book under layers of clothes, snap the padlock shut and shunt the case out of sight. I can't exactly imagine a supernatural being demeaning itself to go scrabbling through manky old sweats to find a long-lost book of angelic wisdom.

I shower and throw on clean clothes. Dad's in the kitchen going through the jobs section. He's circled several ads already.

'Good to see you're on the case,' I say in an encouraging voice.

He doesn't look up. 'If Mike can do it, I can do it.'

'Right. Think positive.'

'I was crazy to think I could just walk back into the restaurant business like some hotshot TV chef. I have to compromise.'

I feel a pang somewhere in my chest, but I try to laugh it off. 'So I guess you're going to take that job as a male stripper after all? That's OK, Dad, we'll still respect you.'

My father looks down at his belly, and gives it a loving pat. 'Listen, my boy, twenty years ago I would have made a stupendous stripper!'

'I refuse to dwell on that picture,' I tell him. 'So if stripping is out, what's the game plan?'

'Basically, I've got to be less macho,' he sighs.

I almost laugh. 'Dad, get real! When have you ever been macho?'

'I've been proud and pigheaded like your mama says.'

'Mum called you pigheaded?' I say disbelievingly. 'No way!'

'It was one of my sisters then!' He beetles his eyebrows. 'We're surrounded by opinionated females,' he says in a stage whisper. 'The fact is there's plenty of jobs in this paper, Dino,' he says in his normal tone. 'They need people to drive minicabs, work behind bars. I just have to be more flexible.'

I want to lie down on the kitchen tiles and howl like a dog.

I want to tell my father I'll rob a bank, *anything*, so he can have his life back. I want to tell him Mike isn't a better man than Dad. Mike isn't even *Mike*! My head is exploding with all I want to say, but can't.

'Going to Zorba's today?' I ask, hating the bland sound of my voice.

'Yeah, yeah,' he says absently. 'Got to pay the bills, you know.'

He calls after me. 'Try to learn something, Konstandino. Then you might not wind up like your old –'

I shut the front door, cutting off the end of the sentence.

I've got absolutely no intention of going to school. I'm already texting Bee, telling her where to meet me.

When I get outside, the headlights are scarcely visible through the fog. People brush past, as anonymous as ghosts.

I don't need Victor Waverley to lecture me on metaphysics this morning. I can feel the change for myself. An invisible tide has turned in the night. You can taste it along with the petrochemicals, the sense of the city rushing headlong into darkness. If I think about it there's a genuine danger I'll fly into a million pieces, so I hurry towards the Underground, shivering and wishing I'd brought a scarf.

A splash of pumpkin-orange jumps out of the gloom. An advertisement for some local Halloween do has been thoughtfully plastered over the pictures of the missing teenager.

When I was a little kid, I used to think bad things only happened to bad people. I don't think that any more. That's why I left the book at home. Anything could happen out in the street. A kid could be mugged, knifed, bundled into a car. The *Book of Light* could vanish for ever. And it would seem normal. Part of the normal senselessness of city life.

The dark entity *has* to know I've got the book. If Waverley's right, it's waiting until the falling light levels reach their lowest point tomorrow at Halloween. If you've been plotting and planning your revenge for close on a thousand years, you wouldn't want any last-minute slip-ups.

But do even Guardians really know how an ancient evil entity ticks? It could be watching me now, purely for amusement. Tracking me through the city like a tiny blip on a screen for absolutely no reason, except that it can.

This thought is so unhinging that for once it's a relief to dive down the Underground. I'm no safer, but I feel illogically less exposed.

I squeeze on to the crowded platform, in time to hear an announcement over the tannoy. Surprise, surprise, there's a delay.

New people push their way on to the platform. Everyone silently shifts along to make room. Minutes drag past. Soon we're all packed together like fruit in a crate.

Each time I feel that sickening tugging on my insides, I edge away. I keep my eyes fixed straight ahead, but I can't do anything about all the cosmic activity whirling and shimmering on the edges of my vision. I'm scared, yet there's a reckless fascination in being this close. Evil is meant to be hideous. But the shadows are disturbingly beautiful, like Tim said.

I feel the faintest vibe, like when someone has been

listening in on your call. No heavy breathing, no click, but you know.

I'm on a crowded platform in a city of millions and something just walked into my mind. I almost lose it. I'm about to spin off, screaming, into the stratosphere with the pure horror of what just happened.

Somehow, don't ask me how, I get my breathing back under control. You knew it could do that, I tell myself. You are not going to play its pervy little mind games. *Let* it read your freaking thoughts! It's a billion-plus years old, it's got to get its thrills somewhere.

There's a blast of foul air and a train comes weaving erratically out of the tunnel. I catch sight of Bee getting out of a carriage. In her hooded parka she could be anyone but I know it's her. I push my way through the crowd and just manage to grab her before she steps on to the escalator. 'Hey!'

Bee spins. Her eyes are enormous under her hood. 'Don't you *ever* do that!'

I hold up my hands. 'Sorry, it was stupid. I was scared you were going to vanish.'

I follow her on to the escalator.

'So are you OK?'

Bee almost laughs. 'In this town? Are you serious?'

'It does feel deeply weird,' I say.

'*Deeply* weird.' Bee shoots me a look from under her hood. 'If I was a religious nut, I might say Armageddon-weird.'

'I forget, is Armageddon like Judgement Day?'

'Kind of like a prequel. Why the indecently early morning texting anyway?'

'Stuff,' I say.

She frowns. 'I'm assuming important stuff, seeing as you made me skip school.'

'Relax, Molloy, if this does turn out to be the coming apocalypse, you could almost definitely get a note.'

'From my mother? Dino, let me tell you, that woman is harsh!'

Our city is turning into a shadowy underworld before our eyes, and what is almost as frightening is we don't even have a basic working vocabulary to describe what's happening.

'Devils' and 'demons' can't do it for us. Not any more. They're like those burned-out celebs who end up in panto wearing tights. The shimmer of meaning that made believers quake in their pews has all been used up. But there's no time to invent new words, so we just ride up the escalator cracking edgy

232

jokes, then we emerge into the eerie half-light and suddenly we stop.

Bee tentatively touches my face. 'Bad night?'

I've been inside her dream. It feels more intimate than sex.

'Strange night,' I tell her. 'You?'

'Roshelle phoned. I couldn't think of a single thing to say. It's like I'm turning into someone I don't even know.' She swallows. 'The only time I don't feel lonely is, rather worryingly, when I'm with you.'

'Ditto,' I say softly.

The fog is steadily growing thicker, blanketing traffic sounds, closing off distances, drawing us into a small ghostly world of our own.

'You had my mobile phone number,' she says, almost whispering.

'Had it a while,' I say.

'Yeah?' She takes a breath. 'So shall we go to Daphne's?'

'Better not. Louis knows my dad.'

'The internet café then?'

It feels like we're the only two human beings heading up the street instead of down. Two school-dodging teenagers amongst the city suits. Two blips of light in a foggy sea of shadows.

The internet café is a warm, brightly lit sanctuary. Bee helps herself to a pastry from the chiller cabinet. 'Breakfast,' she explains with a wan smile.

We've beaten the net freaks today; just an elderly woman with an unusually peaceful face, tapping away, most likely emailing the grandkids.

We find a table out of earshot.

'How was Sadie?' I remember suddenly. It feels as if months have passed since Bee disappeared up the lift shaft with her dad's girlfriend.

'Unbelievably scared.'

'You think she's picking up bad vibes from the Lord of Lies?'

Bee suppresses a shiver. 'She didn't put it like that, but basically yeah. Plus she can't sleep because she's having really violent practice contractions. Too soon to be real, apparently.'

'Is she sure?'

'Positive. They have a proper medical name. Hicks. Bracks or something.' She fiddles nervously with the fake fur on her hood. She looks ridiculously young inside her fashionably huge coat.

'Dino, I'm such a bad person.'

I shake my head. 'Now where did that come from, Molloy?'

'Sadie always seemed like one of those golden people,' she says in a small voice. 'All her life, everything worked out. She thought everybody's life was like that.'

'That must be nice,' I sigh.

'Then when she couldn't get pregnant, you know, *immediately*, she was so shocked and upset. But you know what I thought? I thought, yeah, girl, now you know. But I truly never wanted –'

She breaks off and tries to smile. 'Feel free to shut me up, any time. I know boys hate it when girls get all morbid.'

'Any more news of your dad?'

She shakes her head. 'Not a word. *Nada*. It's just not like him.'

'Isn't it?'

'No, Dino, it isn't! Dad wouldn't run out on her. He's not some monster.'

'Bee, listen, I've got something to tell you. It's kind of bizarre.'

By the time I finish describing how I accidentally eavesdropped on her dream, Bee is squirming. 'God, is *nothing* private!'

'You did great! You didn't buy the big wish-fulfilling fantasy. You told it exactly where to get off.'

'Oh, yippee. Give me a gold star for moral fibre!' she blazes. 'How would you like it if someone came busting into your unconscious, Dino!'

'But it wasn't someone. It was me. And I think there's a reason it was me. Bee, we've got this weird – It's almost like –'

Like magic all the hostility leaves her eyes.

'– telepathy,' she whispers. 'We always did.'

'I know. We've had it for pure time.'

'Then it was like there was this *gap*.' Bee swallows. 'Sometimes I – I wrote you messages.' Her cheekbones flush. 'That must sound really stupid.'

I quickly reach for her hand, and we just look at each other. We don't have to say a word.

For the first time I notice one freaky gold hair at the front, where the hair dye didn't totally take. It makes me stupidly happy.

It's exactly how many days now, since Bee asked me to go with her to the thirteenth floor? I've lost count. It seems weird now the way I couldn't admit that I'd waited for this my whole life.

'That thing you said, that we had to be connected

because of this? I don't understand it,' I say, trying to keep my voice steady. 'But I'd be stupid not to respect it. Even Waverley says so.'

'Sorry, I forgot to ask how that went.' Bee pulls a face. 'Did he sign you up for his bad boys' club?'

I take a breath. 'I was getting round to that.'

Bee listens with growing disbelief. 'No way!' she explodes. 'The guy would have to be like, immortal.'

'I'm not explaining it right. The legends make it seem like there was just the one, but it's actually something that gets passed down through the generations. The outlaw guy, Burbage, was the first. And James Wilkins, he was one.'

'Then he's a liar! He said he hadn't even seen the book!'

'No, he said he hadn't read the *rules*.'

I see her silently digesting this.

'You believe it, don't you?' she says at last. 'You believe Victor is the Guardian.'

'He's different down there, Bee. If you'd seen him you'd know what I mean. It's like he taps into this –'

She claps her hands over her ears. 'Don't say "the Force" or I'll have to punch you!'

I can't help grinning. 'I was going to say "authority"!' I correct her.

I take a super-deep breath and tell her about us having joint responsibility for the book, and the added pressure of Halloween.

Bee looks dazed. 'I don't know which is more bizarre. Mum's loser boyfriend being the Guardian, or Tim being a trainee warrior.'

My mobile starts to vibrate in my hip pocket. I want to ignore it, but something makes me take the call.

'Flowers? You're not at school either! Civilisation is –'

Tim's voice is so low I can hardly make out the words.

'There's this little park, between Paris Gardens and Monkwell Alley. Meet me there, OK?'

I put my phone away. My lungs feel funny. It's like suddenly I can't get enough air. 'Something's happened,' I tell Bee.

Tim is on a swing, scooting himself gently to and fro. With his head tucked in and his elbows sticking out on either side of the chains, he reminds me of those sad birds that were never actually designed to fly.

Bee makes a little sound of distress and I squeeze her hand, but it's really me I'm trying to comfort. And

I'm wondering if maybe they take time to get a hold. The dark shimmer is so faint, I could almost make myself believe it was an optical illusion, if it wasn't for his eyes; the missing spark I'm noticing only now that it's gone.

We push open the kiddies' safety gate and he looks up quite calmly.

'Hi, thanks for coming,' he says politely.

You git, Skerakis, I tell myself.

Did it even occur to you that something might have happened to *him*, on the thirteenth floor, while you were gone?

Dino, we just got here. And I went along with it; even told myself he'd got off lightly, and all the time . . .

I could have saved him last night. Last night he was still putting up a struggle.

'Why, man?' I demand huskily. 'Why'd you do it?'

He shoots a look at Bee. 'She knows.'

She still can't make her voice work; she has to clear her throat and try again. 'Persia,' she says.

'You did this so you could get a *girl*? Are you insane?'

He smiles. 'You think I didn't know I was a joke? I could have a black belt in every fighting style going and I'd still be a joke.'

There's no bitterness, that's what gets me. Just this deeply disturbing calm that makes me want to knock him off his swing.

'Tim, who bloody cares what people at school think? You're worth any number of those morons!'

'I care!' he says quietly. 'Everyone cares, even if they don't show it. The fact is, you never had to worry about it. I wanted to feel like that, Dino. I wanted to feel that confident even just once.'

'But this isn't even real, man! That – that *thing* can make Persia act like she cares about you, but you'll always know it isn't real!'

'So what if it isn't real! What's real anyway? I just want to be happy.'

'Tim, trust me, this is not how happiness looks.'

'It is to me,' he says stubbornly. 'She's beautiful. I've got everything I ever wanted.'

'Everything you ever wanted. Right.'

'I just thought you should know,' he says. 'I thought you ought to know how things were.'

I'm dangerously close to bawling my eyes out. 'So that's why you phoned? Like a courtesy call? Am going to hell – may be gone some time?'

He's talking over me. 'I need you to tell Mr

Waverley I won't be coming to the training sessions any more.'

'Tim, don't shut him out! He's the Guardian, man! If anyone can understand, it's him.'

Tim glances at his watch. He lets his shoes scuff along the ground, and slows the swing to a halt. 'I've got to go. She's waiting.'

We watch him walk across the park and out through the gates.

I notice that his painful self-consciousness has totally gone. I guess when you've got a black hole instead of a soul, the worst has already happened.

'The others are lucky,' I say bitterly. 'They have no idea what they've done to themselves. Tim knows.'

'He still shouldn't be wandering round the city like that.' Bee takes out her phone, sniffing back tears. 'When is Halloween anyway?'

I'm staring miserably after Tim. 'Tomorrow, why?'

'He definitely shouldn't then.' She viciously punches out a number. 'I hate it when I have to eat my words,' she says. 'I HATE it!'

'Who are you calling?'

'Ssh, I'm concentrating. Oh, hi! Can you tell me if Mr Waverley will be in today, please?'

I have no clue what she's up to, but I would prefer it if I didn't have to see Victor Waverley. That water lily speech sounded like pure gobbledegook last night. But now I understand what he couldn't bring himself to say in so many words.

You tipped the balance. Dino. You.

I virtually delivered Tim to the thirteenth floor, like a disposable sidekick in a movie. Funny old Supergeek – so insignificant, the audience won't even notice when he's gone.

Waverley knew Tim wasn't strong enough to handle it. He guessed what would happen.

'Sorry, what did you say your name was?' Bee rings off looking stunned. 'You'll never believe who just answered the phone.'

'Who?' I say, not much caring.

'Mimi Rousseau.'

CHAPTER 12

'SHORTCUTS,' says Mimi, briskly wiping down tables. 'Everyone's into shortcuts. Everyone wants something and no one wants to wait. He uses that. He makes you feel like it's owing to you. He's the ultimate – oh, hi, Terry!'

A painfully thin guy in a hoodie is hovering. 'Mimi, I got this nasty blister.'

We're back in the church, sitting at one of the formica-topped tables. By night it's the boys' club. In daylight hours it's a local drop-in centre for the homeless.

Mimi unlocks the first-aid cabinet and gives Terry a plaster for his heel. The drop-in centre smells pretty much how you'd expect. Dirty clothes, stale booze, mentholated chest rub.

In contrast, Mimi Rousseau reeks of cleanliness. Her skin is literally shiny with soap. I guess, once you've lived on the streets, you could never really feel too clean.

'We've got some nice soup,' she tells Terry. 'Plus

Marks and Sparks sent a batch of yesterday's sandwiches. Get yourself some dinner, yeah, and we'll see if we can find you some better shoes.' She shakes her head. 'What was I saying again? Oh, yeah. He's like the ultimate – what's that phrase, Victor?'

'Loan shark,' he supplies quietly.

I shift nervously in my seat. Waverley's hardly said a word to me since I told him about Tim. He didn't say much then, just shot off into a corner and talked urgently on his mobile, then came back and continued helping Mimi.

We've been here approximately half an hour, and I'm still struggling to square the new Mimi with the sexy-vulnerable icon in crumpled lace. If she wore her hair loose, maybe, but the wholesome little scrunchy plus the scrubbed complexion makes her look disconcertingly like some brisk staff nurse.

'Yeah, the ultimate loan shark,' she muses. 'A little twist here. A little twiddle there. By the time you realise he's playing you like a tuba, it's too late. You're screwed. Pass me those mugs, will you, darling?' She works as she talks, calmly collecting dirty crockery, stacking it on her tray.

Bee looks as bewildered as I feel. Neither of us can

understand why Mimi Rousseau, local wild child and rock chick, is slumming down at the homeless centre. She's *had* her Cinderella period, waiting on tables, living in bedsits. Then she got her big break. This girl used to go on world tours. She sang with all the best artists. She was set to live happily and famously ever after.

'But *Souls for Sale* is like the ultimate concept album,' Bee blurts out. 'I still listen to it all the time. That lyric "nothing lasts but everything matters". I get goosebumps every time I hear it.'

'*Screwed*,' Mimi repeats firmly.

'But what happened?' Bee sounds genuinely distressed.

Mimi smiles. 'To my fabulous career? For one thing my agent slipped up big time over the royalties. Of course, by then I'd spent them twice over. Comes expensive, being a celeb.' She gives a little spurt of laughter. 'Celeb! I ask you! The original one-hit wonder, that's me.'

'Don't you *mind*?' I ask.

'Not any more, darling,' she says. 'I'm too grateful.'

I try to imagine what I'd feel if my life crashed in flames like a hijacked plane. I'm pretty sure it wouldn't be gratitude.

'Listen, Dino, here's how it works. You make a deal.

He fixes your problem. The boyfriend or girlfriend comes back. You get the job. You get the big contract. Name in pretty pink lights, whatever. Bam. Sorted. It's finally Christmas. Only it's not real, is it? It doesn't last. It can't.'

Souls for Sale was real, I think.

'Plus there's a sneaky kickback he conveniently forgets to mention,' she adds casually.

I feel a sharp lurch in my belly. 'What kind of kickback?'

Mimi sits down, and drags her hair more firmly into her scrunchy.

'All those old problems you couldn't solve first time around? They come boomeranging back, only ten times worse. After *Souls for Sale* came out, I went through stuff that made my old troubles look like lemon drops.'

'The price is too high,' someone repeats behind me.

It's the ranting drunk from the traffic lights.

Mimi laughs. 'Change the CD, Douggie, there's a love.'

He carries his mug of tea over to a table, still mumbling.

'But how – I mean, you sold your –'

Bee's voice trails off. Mimi looks about a million years old suddenly. Earthquake victims look like that.

People who've been through indescribable horrors. Mimi's young and talented. No way should she be here in the homeless centre with those eyes.

She tries to smile. 'Here's the thing you need to understand, both of you. When you make a deal, it's like – you're kind of giving him the right to say what's real.'

I sneak an uneasy glance at Waverley.

'Was it horrible?' Bee asks in a scared voice. 'Getting it back?'

Mimi shakes her head. 'You don't want to know, darling, believe me.' She quickly puts her hand over Bee's. 'You're worried about your dad, aren't you?'

'He just disappeared. No one has any idea where he's gone. I'm scared something's happened.'

Mimi shoots a look at Waverley. 'Tell her, man.'

'He's safe,' he tells Bee in a tired voice.

'You know where he is!' Bee jumps up. 'I've got to go and see him!'

He shakes his head. 'Your father's in a pretty confused state. It's better if you don't see him just now.'

'Don't try to fob me off, all right? Sadie's having their baby any minute. She needs to know he's OK. We all do. He *is* OK, isn't he?'

'Victor,' Mimi warns. 'She isn't a child. She deserves to know.'

There's a prickly silence. Waverley pushes back his chair.

'I warn you, you're going to find it disturbing.'

I go to follow, but Mimi yanks me back into my seat. 'This is between Bee and her dad.'

While they're gone, we chat about music. I ask Mimi if she's heard the new remix of 'Nothing Lasts'. 'There must be royalties knocking around for that, surely?' I say.

'Dino, try to understand,' she says. 'I got a second chance. Everything else is gravy. I don't care about all that stuff any more.'

'That's *it*? From now on the drop-in centre is going to be like, your entire universe?'

She pats my arm, almost like she feels sorry for me.

'The drop-in centre is an OK place actually, Dino. It's all right here. Everyone knows the score. Those terrors that keep normal people awake at nights, those things people think they couldn't survive – we've been there. We've been to hell and back. But we did survive. We're not the same; we'll never ever be the same. But we *survived*, that's the thing.'

248

But you're a singer, I think. You should be singing, man.

If I close my eyes I can still hear the gritty-sweet voice that made 'Nothing Lasts' a runaway chart-topper for an entire summer.

'No disrespect,' I say, 'but there's more to life than surviving.'

She gives me her million-year-old smile. 'I used to think like that. I was so busy trying to get somewhere, trying to be somebody, I missed the point. I never want to do that again.'

I want to tell her to stop coming on like freaking Buddha and do what she was born to do. 'So what is the point exactly?' I say nastily.

Mimi's used to this. People thinking she's let them down.

'I can't say what it is for you, Dino. It's just little things for me. Having a friendly chat with someone. Showing him he matters.'

'Do-gooding,' I say.

'Being kind,' she says softly.

Waverley and Bee come back. Bee is barely holding herself together. Waverley looks furious. 'Dino, I'm going to ask you to give me the book back,' he says.

I feel a pang, an actual physical pain inside. Last night I was the joint keeper of the *Book of Light*. Now he doesn't trust me, because of what happened to Tim.

'I haven't got it,' I tell him. 'It's at home.'

'You went off and *left* it?'

'I thought it would be safer – I thought –'

'Go back and get it.'

'But I –'

'NOW!' he barks.

'I'll come with you.' I hear a quiver in Bee's voice.

'After I bring it back, then what?' I ask Waverley.

'I'm not sure. We have to find another way. It's not you, Dino, it's me,' he says quickly. 'I realised I couldn't – I can't let you kids take the risk. Get back here as soon as you can, OK? And don't go doing anything stupid, either of you.'

My stomach muscles unclench.

Waverley isn't angry. He's done what a Guardian is not supposed to do. He got involved; he cares what happens to us, me and Bee. He cares too much.

Bee looks so wiped that when we get outside I take her hand without thinking. 'Girl, you're freezing!'

'No, I'm OK.'

We hurry along, hand in hand, through the fog.

'So what's the story with your old man?'

She gives me a strained smile. 'Remember Tina's story about a maze of old tunnels under the city? It turns out they're true.'

'They've got your *dad* in a tunnel?'

'You know what's weird? I've been dreaming about them, I've been dreaming hideous tunnel dreams since this started.'

'Me too,' I say huskily.

'The Guardians have this safe place down there, where they put people who – basically, their own minds are driving them crazy. Victor only has the manpower and resources to help a few. But he has these really good people taking care of them, trying to – to undo –' Bee makes a distressed little gesture. 'Can't talk about it, sorry.'

She's broken into my dream, the part I didn't want to remember. The wild-eyed faces peering out through iron bars, the frantic voices promising me the moon if only I'll set them free.

Her lip quivers. 'Dad didn't even know who I was. When I went in, he said, "You're a smart girl, I can tell. Think you could put a bet on the 2.30 for me? Magic Princess. It's a sure thing."'

We were the cool kids, the popular kids. We'd brush past each other in the corridor, flanked by our respective crews; Dino Skerakis and Bee Molloy. The stubble-headed basketball player and the gorgeous princess.

Now, like antelope on the plains, we've been split off not just from our former friends, but from everything we thought we were.

'I've got something to tell you,' Bee says in a low voice as we walk into Mortagaine House. 'Victor says he knows you're not going to like it. He wants to keep us somewhere safe until Halloween is over.'

There is no safe place, not any more, but I just call the lift.

'Who's us?' I ask her.

'You, me, Sadie, the book. It would just be for twenty-four hours, until Halloween's come and gone.'

'How do you plan to explain it to Sadie?'

'You saw how she was. She knows something isn't right.'

We ride up in the lift in silence. The instant we step out on to my landing, I feel a vibe that has nothing to do with magic.

Our front door is standing open, I can hear my mother on the phone.

'No, Tippie, I'm trying to explain. When they saw the results they said they had to keep him in. I just came back for his things. They don't know, lovie. They think they could have caught it in time but the fact is they don't know.'

Bee and I are frozen behind the door.

'I'm just going back now. I'll phone as soon as I – no, lovie, don't feel you have to. I wouldn't dream of putting you through that. Yes, thank you, that means a lot. Bye, lovie.'

Bee deliberately lets the door slam

My mother comes out of the bedroom, suspiciously red around the eyes. She sees me, and immediately looks guilty. 'Shouldn't you two be at school?' she says quickly.

'Why didn't you say Dad was having tests?' My voice sounds like it belongs to someone else.

Mum starts fussing with Dad's overnight bag. 'We thought you'd been through enough,' she says in a muffled voice. 'Dad wouldn't want you to upset yourself. He'll be fine. Really he will. I'll call you as soon as there's any news. Lovely to meet you, erm, Beatrice, isn't it?'

'Bee,' says Bee, swallowing. 'Everyone calls me Bee.'

I watch numbly as my mother walks out of the flat and into the lift.

We thought you'd been through enough.

My dad could be dying and I never even knew. They've been protecting me, just like a child.

Bee touches my arm. 'Tell me where you put the book. I'll get it!'

I stare at her. I'm not sure what she just said. The massiveness of what's happening makes me feel totally spaced.

'I'll get it for you,' she repeats.

With enormous effort, I drag myself back. 'No, it's easier if I do.'

'Meet you downstairs then. Sadie's flat's on the third floor near the fire exit. Take the stairs, OK? I'm going to.'

The book is where I left it. I don't even feel relief, just zip it inside my jacket. On my way out, I hear the TV in the kitchen talking to itself. I go in to turn it off. A guy is telling the studio audience he hasn't been unfaithful, but a lie detector test reveals he lied. The audience boos and hisses but no one really cares.

I take the stairs, jogging numbly from landing to landing. It's getting dark and the stairwell is full of shadows. I could turn on the lights, but what really would be the point?

I bang on Sadie's door. 'Bee, it's me.'

She takes ages to answer. I assume she's helping Sadie pack her stuff, so I just lean my forehead on the wall.

At last the door opens. Bee pulls me in and shuts the door. 'I had to call the ambulance,' she says in a low voice. 'The baby's coming.'

I can see Sadie through an open door. She's sitting bolt upright on the edge of her chair, as if she's about to be interviewed. There's this weird expression on her face, like she's listening to something far far away.

'Isn't it too soon?' I whisper.

Sadie lets out a sudden animal moan. 'Bee! Could you call them again and tell them to hurry!'

'They're on their way, sweetheart. Try to hang on a little bit longer.'

Bee makes soothing noises to her dad's girlfriend, as if she's talking to a scared little sister, until the paramedics come. They wear brightly coloured clothing, like some form of extreme hiking gear.

'Think you can walk to the lift, darling?' says the woman. They try to help Sadie to her feet, but she just collapses.

'I can't!' she wails. 'Something terrible is happening. I can feel it.'

'First baby?' the woman asks Bee.

She gives a frightened nod.

'Thought so,' grins the woman. 'They're all drama queens the first time.'

They lift her on to a stretcher and we crowd into the service lift. When we arrive at the ground floor, they wheel Sadie out.

Bee's eyes are glassy with fear. She clutches at my hand. 'We're too late. We haven't found the rules. He's going to take her baby, Dino.'

'That isn't going to happen,' I tell her. 'It's all going to be OK.'

'How do you know?'

I put my arms around her. 'I know, trust me.'

'I'd better go with her,' Bee whispers. 'She shouldn't be on her own, not now. You'd better take the book to Waverley.'

'Sure,' I say. 'I'll go down there right away.'

I watch the ambulance drive away, lights flashing, siren blaring. I watch it disappear into the fog, then wait a moment longer, listening to the frantic siren shrieking up Monkwell Street.

Then I walk inside Mortagaine House and call the lift.

I can't save the world. I can't even help my own dad. But I can do this. I get in and I smash my fist into the control panel.

'Guess what, dickhead!' I call up the shaft. 'Halloween came early. I'm coming on up!'

For a long moment nothing happens, then an enormous shudder goes through the cage.

All the buttons on the panel light up.

Making absolutely no sound, the lift starts to move.

CHAPTER 13

I'M no longer scared, that's the strange thing.

Waverley says I wasn't chosen. Well, bollocks to that. What if *I* choose? What if I choose myself? I've had enough of playing kiss-chase with the bogeyman, dancing to some antiquated tune written before the dawn of time.

I'm not disrespecting Waverley. He's doing a great job, saving damaged kids, rescuing people from their own insanity, but he can't save us – probably no one can. But I'm damned if I'm going to hide away like some little girl.

I don't try to guess what I'll see when the lift doors open. It'll only be something he's borrowed from overheated human imaginations. Zombie kids with barcodes. Supernatural clubs where you get to score a glamorous new life in return for your soul. He's been playing us for centuries. Not any more.

The lift stops so smoothly, it takes a few seconds to

realise I've arrived. Before I can touch it, the gate slides back as silently as if it's been oiled. I step out, totally wired, and almost fall over a boy in a bellhop's uniform.

'You're expected,' he smirks.

'You *know* that,' I say grimly in my street voice.

It's a warm summer evening in an old-fashioned hotel. Wide-open windows let in a pleasant breeze. Chandeliers tinkle over my head and, as I follow the fake bellboy along the carpeted corridor, I can hear distant sounds of jazz and laughter, a soundtrack to a party that doesn't exist.

The book has started to become supernaturally heavy inside my jacket. By the time the bellboy stops in front of an imposing panelled door, I feel as if my spine is going to crack. But I know this is just another of Mr Nobody's conjuring tricks.

The bellhop seems to be waiting for a tip.

'You are joking,' I growl.

And he vanishes like a soap bubble.

I go to turn the handle then stop, unnerved. The oak panels are carved with deeply disturbing images. The longer I look, the more it seems like the monstrous scaly creatures are on the verge of coming alive.

'Same tired old spooky FX,' I say out loud. 'Snakes,

gruesome. Winged horrors, various.'

I'm trying to buy extra time. Pure fury got me up here. Now I need something solid. A plan for instance.

The monsters seem to read my mind. One rears two of its three hideous heads with sudden interest. The third head hisses like a cobra.

'Are you going to open this?' I yell. 'Or have I got to kick this piece of junk down?'

The heads retract silently into the oak.

The double doors slowly fold inwards.

I'm so psyched up, I'm prepared for anything. When they finally reveal a completely empty room, I'm almost disappointed.

I walk over to the window. I can hear my own footsteps echoing on polished marble. A tense-seeming boy looks back at me from the glass.

'Now what?' I ask him.

A second reflection materialises silently beside the first.

I was prepared for anything except this horror.

I turn – every molecule in my body time-lapse slow – until I'm looking into the face of a boy who hasn't been seen for twenty years.

His clothes are different to the news photos, but the

look in his eyes still gives me goosebumps.

My heart is thumping in my throat, but I can't let him see I'm scared. 'You're not Martin,' I tell him. 'Martin Coombs is dead.'

He laughs. 'I'm more alive than the boy in those pictures ever was.'

'Lurking up here, picking off small children like an evil spider is not what I'd describe as being alive,' I say in disgust. 'What did you offer the poor kid? A truckload of sweeties? His own personal skateboard park?'

He winces. 'You wouldn't talk like that if you knew the truth.'

'So did you do him in personally? Or did you happen across a nice warm corpse and decide you might as well crawl in out of the cold?'

The boy's eyes widen with convincing alarm. The big rough boy is scaring him. 'What they've told you is lies,' he says. 'But that's OK, because you're here now and that's what matters.'

I stare at him. 'You *wanted* to meet me? Me, personally?'

'Only for a thousand years,' he grins. 'There were times I thought it would never happen, believe me.'

Not only has this Martin got the compact wiry body of a healthy ten-year-old, he has the fidgety boyish mannerisms and voice perfectly. Seeing him, I almost sense what the real Martin was like.

I give a disbelieving laugh. 'You want me to believe you've been waiting a thousand years for this moment? Yeah, right. So your thirteenth-floor project was really just an evil little hobby to kill time until I rocked up outside your door?'

'It's not a hobby,' he says with a ten-year-old's injured dignity. 'Where we're standing now, it's like the – the hub of the cosmos. Have you any idea what that means?'

'Not a clue, but it sounds deeply head-trippy.'

'I suppose I knew it would take time for you to trust me,' he sighs.

'*Trust* you! You are a piece of work, you know that? You're trying to destroy everyone's lives and you want me to *trust* you!'

He looks bewildered. 'Is that what they've been telling you?'

'I didn't need anyone to tell me, dickhead, I have eyes!' I push my face close to his. 'Listen, you little gob of slime, all humans are not the same. You're not going to buy me, or Bee, and you don't lay a finger on her baby sister or Sadie. So you can unplug your cosmic hub from

262

the mains and crawl back into whatever stinking hellhole you came from. It's OVER!' By this time I'm yelling in his face.

'You could just ask. You don't have to yell.' Martin's eyes brim with tears. He looks so pitiful, I could believe it was for real.

'OK, supposing we forget for now that you punched a million-plus holes in our reality. Forget that you've ruined a million-plus lives. We'll even forget what you did to my family and just focus on the Molloys. Over the past week, you have pushed Bee's dad over the edge, terrorised his girlfriend. For all I know you're trying to harm their unborn kid at this moment – and you expect me to believe you'll stop because I come upstairs and ASK you nicely?'

He shakes his head. He looks genuinely despairing. 'If you'd give me a chance I could explain, but you're just so prejudiced. You've made up your mind I'm this alien creature, but I'm really just like you.'

'I am nothing like you, dirtbag. NOTHING!'

'My reality might have a couple more dimensions than you're used to, but I want all the same things you want,' he insists.

'Isn't there an expiry date for you people? Because it

looks like you've got a serious senility situation. Don't you get it? While you're up here in cosmic lala-land, real people are suffering!'

He ducks his head tearfully as if my words have hit home. 'I know. I *know*. And I want to put all that right, truly. But it would be much easier if you'd just keep an open mind. I'm not trying to trick you, but I need to show you who I really am, and I can't do it unless you trust me.'

'OK, Bat Boy,' I say coolly. 'Amaze me with your phenomenal superpowers.'

I want to see how long he can keep up this act of being the cute little brother I never had.

His face lights up like a Christmas tree. He brushes tears from his lashes. 'You *really* want to see what I can do?'

'I said so, didn't I?' I growl. 'So where are we going? Toys R Us?'

Martin laughs his sweet kid's laugh. 'Everywhere and nowhere! Don't look so mad. Just take my hand. It's safe, I'm not going to hurt you.'

He smells of sunshine and shampoo. His hand in mine feels almost like a normal hand – warm, slightly sweaty.

'You're going to love this,' he beams. 'I'm going to show you the world you could be living in.'

I'm walking through the city with a murdered boy.

The hardest thing is trying to keep the awe out of my face because this is so not how I expected it to feel.

When Bee and I walked through the streets to Mortagaine House, the dying light made the city seem like a ghostly graveyard of human hopes and dreams. But when you see through the eyes of a multi-dimensional being, you can burn through that and I'm sorry, but it's beautiful!

Half these colours I've never even seen before. I've certainly never heard people's thoughts surging around me like the hum of some huge beehive. Shouldn't I be scared? Shouldn't it feel creepy to be mingling with people who don't know we're there?

It doesn't. It feels magic. The way we're slightly out of synch with our surroundings, moving fractionally too slowly and gracefully, like boy gods in jeans, actually heightens the feeling of enchantment. It feels strangely familiar, almost as if I'm reliving an event that has already happened.

I glance suspiciously at the hyperactive ten-year-old

bounding along beside me. 'You wouldn't be messing with time by any chance?'

Martin laughs. 'Forget about time. Time is nothing. I'm going to show you something that will blow you away.' He starts to tug me through the unrecognisably magical streets. 'What's your favourite building?'

'Are you five?' I say irritably. 'I don't have a favourite building.'

'OK, pick one at random. Somewhere you'd never normally go.'

You'd expect an evil entity to be jaded and cynical, but he's buzzing, like a kid who's consumed too many chemical additives. We happen to be passing a bank, so I say wearily, 'The vaults?'

'Perfect!' Martin grabs my hand and pulls me through a dizzy succession of walls and floors, until we're standing in a hushed shrine of steel and polished wood that literally reeks of money.

I'm stunned, as he knew I would be. 'That has to be the weirdest sensation. No, it's *way* to the left of weird.'

'Want to do it slower? You see the particles then!'

For Martin, or, more accurately, the entity currently impersonating Martin, matter is simply an illusion. Solid buildings become a shimmer of atoms, the instant he wants to see what's going on inside. We play with this concept for a while, then he drags me down into the Underground so I can watch him do his big party trick, morphing fearlessly backwards and forwards from one high-speed train into another.

I turn away. I don't care if he is a multidimensional being, impervious to being physically squashed. I just can't look.

Eventually he gets bored playing with trains and drags me into a concert hall where a famous chamber orchestra is rehearsing. Martin says he loves classical music, and, as we listen in the dark auditorium, I feel the strangest sensation, as if the cellos and violins are changing something inside me. They're changing something in Martin too. I can see it in his eyes: a painful longing, as if the swooping sounds remind him of something lost and gone for ever.

Then BAM! he's back in hyperactive mode.

'Come on! I'm going to show you my best thing!'

Martin's best thing turns out to be riding up in a builder's cradle, till we reach the top of what will be the city's tallest skyscraper, when it's finished. We perch side by side on an overhanging girder, like some surreal remake of Huck Finn and Tom Sawyer.

The city looks shockingly beautiful from here. I should be cold, but I can't seem to feel a thing except this child-like pleasure. I could sit, gazing down like this, for hours. Perhaps we do, because after a while the sun starts to set, and the sky slowly fills with wonderful frozen colours. I wonder vaguely what time it is, then realise I don't even know if it's the same day.

'Want a piece of gum?' Martin thrusts a packet under my nose.

'No way! I'm not taking gum from you!'

'It's just gum, Dino!'

'Don't use my name. And again, no way,' I tell him firmly.

I look at him dangling his legs over a several-thousand-feet drop, looking totally at home. 'I'm guessing devils don't suffer from vertigo?'

He smiles. 'SSh, listen! Their thoughts sound so cool up here.'

I note the flattering upgrade. He's encouraging me to think of myself as an honorary immortal.

Martin makes an almost-casual gesture.

The din from the streets below changes; certain sounds fade, others grow sharper and more resonant. Now I can make out individual voices, some pleading, some weeping, all obsessively going over and over the same thing.

'What are we going to do?' one woman keeps asking distractedly. 'What in the world are we going to do now?'

I shake my head in disgust. 'You love that, don't you? All that suffering; knowing you're the cause. It gives you a pervy little buzz.'

'I'll turn it down if it bothers you.' He makes another gesture, and the voices fade, merging seamlessly into the background beehive hum.

Martin's face is almost tender. 'Don't you think it sounds just like music? Up here everything always looks and sounds so beautiful and nothing ever hurts.'

Something cold trickles down my spine.

Is Martin deliberately playing me back my own thoughts? Or is he genuinely trying to share his own?

'Sometimes I think I like it best at night,' he says in his new tender voice. 'When all the lights come on, the patterns are quite mathematical. They give an illusion of order and harmony that's totally missing in your world by day. Then times like now, I think the sunsets are the best. Polluted skies make the best sunsets, did you know that?'

He's not even trying to talk like Martin now. And the expression, playing over his unnaturally young features, is nothing like Martin's smile.

He glances at his watch, I hadn't noticed he was wearing one until now; it's the old-fashioned kind with numbers set around a dial. A glittering hand crawls infinitely slowly from numeral to numeral.

I wonder what units a being like Martin might need to measure. Centuries? Aeons?

He laughs and shows me his watch. Where a manufacturer's name should be, it says simply ETERNITY.

'I'm not after the book,' he says. 'Really, why would I need it?'

I'm increasingly uneasy. I don't know whether to believe him. But really, why would he?

'So what's all this been about? As a matter of interest?'

'I already told you! To meet you! To share all this with you.'

He lifts his arms as if he's going to dance. I feel something surge down into the city and a million-plus lights go on, not one at a time but in sparkling strings and loops like jewellery.

'It's only ever been about you,' he says tenderly.

There's another surge, and the far-off ebb and flow of sound down below acquires a familiar trippy bass line.

I feel dizzy. He wants me to see what it would be like to have this kind of power. How you could play with reality, mixing time, space, light, sounds, human pain and suffering. He's showing me that it's really the devil who's the ultimate DJ.

'I'm not the devil,' he says as if I'd spoken aloud. 'You keep saying I'm the devil.' He glances again at the glittering hand flicking through the nameless unknown units of eternity.

I feel a creeping chill seep into my bones. 'Then what –?'

'It's hardly relevant now,' he says.

Martin gets to his feet in one smooth athletic movement and kills the sounds. The new silence rushes into my ears, making me feel deaf.

He balances on the girder, arms outstretched, like a boy gymnast. 'Want to see your dad?' he says in his friendly ten-year-old's voice. 'We can drop in on him, see how he's doing? You must be worried.'

I'm in a hospital corridor under harsh white lights. Nurses and porters emerge through swing doors, propelling a trolley with an urgency that until now I've only seen on TV. My mother is half running to keep up, clasping the hand of the unconscious man under the blanket. 'He's going to be all right, isn't he?' she pleads. 'He is going to be all right?'

Then we're back in the empty room on the thirteenth floor. Actually, now we're back, I'm not sure we were ever really outside. Words like 'real' and 'unreal', 'inside' and 'outside' used to mean something once.

I'm sick and trembling, because of what I've just seen and because of what is just about to happen.

Up till a few seconds ago, Martin wanted me to think I had the advantage. Now every nerve in my body is telling me I'm the prey.

'You made your point. You have the power, dirtbag. Now what?'

Martin keeps his eyes fixed hungrily on the glowing hand ticking around the dial. 'Five, four, three,' he murmurs. 'Two, one –'

The watch face lights up with a sickly green glow, illuminating his face disturbingly from below.

Outside the windows, the enchanted colours fade to monochrome.

He lets out a peal of laughter. 'Happy Halloween, Dino!'

I look into his eyes and it feels like drowning in darkness.

I'm seeing him as he really is. The shadow behind the shadows. The Lord of Lies himself.

Everything he said, everything he showed me, was leading to this moment. Pure delaying tactics to kill time while the light levels dropped. I can't believe I fell for it.

'So take it,' I say shakily. 'Take my freaking soul and make my dad well again.'

He actually laughs. 'No offence, but I think we both know Dino Skerakis's immortal soul is not the prize which has kept me bound to this earth for a thousand years.'

I'm frantic. 'What else have I got you could possibly want?'

'A long time ago,' he says, 'I made a mistake. I fell, and now I can't stop falling. You could say it's a paradox. We thirst for the beauty we've lost, but we can't get it back so, to find peace, we're forced to destroy the very thing we long for.'

I force myself to meet his eyes. 'I call that hell,' I tell him.

It's Halloween. The balance of power has fatally shifted in his favour. Yet for some reason I'm still putting up a fight. 'So when you said you didn't need the book, that was a "paradox", right? It wasn't just an outright, you know, lie?'

He shrugs. 'Does it matter?'

He's acquired a long coat from somewhere. It makes him look older, more like a dark angel. His trainers glow in the dusk like burning coals. I wonder if it's even true what he just told me. I guess he'd say that didn't matter.

'Suppose you were to get hold of the *Book of Light*,' I say, as if we don't both know I have it zipped inside my jacket, 'what happens then?'

He smiles and again I see that whirling darkness in his eyes.

'I'll be free.'

'Surprisingly, I wasn't talking about you. I meant all those people down there.'

'Your family will be fine. That's all that matters, right?'

I picture the long line of Guardians reaching back through the centuries. All that patient training and instilling of discipline. I think of the secret legends passed on in whispers under tables and in boarded-up houses, so the kids of the future would know how to defend themselves against the inhuman being on the thirteenth floor.

Now the future is here and there isn't one magic rule, one word dictated by an angel that can save us.

Suddenly all the fight drains out of me. I feel totally empty. I've been trying to believe like Bee, but when you get down to it, each of us is alone. My dad could be dying. What else can I do?

The DJ temptation must have just been for practice. A dry run, so he'd know how much pressure to apply to make a cocky teenage boy cave in. He got it just right. Everyone has a bottom line, and this is mine.

Martin knows he's won, of course he does, but he needs to hear me say it. That's how he relieves some of that burning poison he carries inside.

I can see the glow of his trainers reflecting in his eyes. My throat aches, and I know I've finally run out of road.

'OK,' I whisper. 'It's a deal.'

I wish my heart had stopped beating, the night I gatecrashed Bee's dream. Then I'd never have found out what a jerk I really am; storming up to the thirteenth floor like a big action hero, when really I'm no different to all the others. Like everyone else, I have a price.

To deepen the humiliation, I can't seem to unfasten the zip on my jacket. I zipped it up in too much of a hurry. Now the teeth have completely bent out of shape. I stand there, frantically jiggling the tiny metal tag; the ape boy who can't even work a zip fastener.

You'd think he'd zap me with his dark powers, to speed things up. But I guess postponing the pleasure just makes it sweeter, because he can't resist milking his moment of triumph just a tiny bit more.

'I will be taking your soul, obviously,' he remarks casually.

I have a fleeting image of a store room stashed full of lost souls. But there's nothing left to feel.

'I never really knew what the deal was with souls,' I tell him. 'I guess now I'll find out.'

I've managed to free the zip but Martin doesn't seem to notice.

'Would you like me to *tell* you the deal, Dino?' he says. 'So you'll understand exactly what I'm taking away from you?'

'Would it really matter if I said no?'

He laughs. 'FACT. Every human has one, but most people never notice, unless something happens to activate it. FACT. Souls are activated by intense experiences, also by music or other art forms, but most of all by the proximity of another soul to whom you have a special connection. You must have noticed that when you're with Bee, the world suddenly had more colours.'

'Shut up about her,' I say. 'Don't even dare say her name.'

'You might be interested to know that it was the combined power of your two souls which activated the *Book of Light*. FACT,' he goes on relentlessly. 'Your soul contains in coded form not just everything you ever were, and everything you are, but everything you have the potential to be. FACT. There isn't one of you pathetic whingeing humans who won't hand theirs over in a flash for the price of a hot meal or a fat cheque the moment life gets just a little bit sticky.'

I've stopped listening. Martin's jeering voice fades harmlessly into the background and I didn't need to make a magical gesture. He's just told me I'm not alone.

A wave of pure joy goes through me. *I'm not alone!*

I remember how it feels to dance for hours in a crowded club, all of us in the mix together, pulling down the sounds. The way it feels to be running around the court with the basketball when for no apparent reason the game starts to play through you.

I don't just remember these things, I see them. I FEEL them in every tiny electrically charged cell.

I see Dad in his hideous synthetic sweater, beetling his black brows, confidently informing me that garlic will boost my sex life.

And in the café with Bee, how she looked at me when I said we were destined to meet up. I feel that. Most of all I feel that.

It isn't the *Book of Light* that links us. It's the universe itself. The beautiful messed-up universe of divine sounds and dog-dirt, human souls and suffering.

That's how we were able to survive the toxic darkness of the thirteenth floor, and wake up an angelic text that had lain dormant for almost a thousand years.

That's why, at this moment, I'm electrically connected not just to Bee but to everyone who ever stood where I'm standing now. I can literally feel them crowding into the room, jostling and whispering expectantly. They all seem to be waiting for me to do something, so I do.

I do the only thing that's left. The one totally unthinkable thing.

'Catch!' I yell and I pitch the book straight at Martin. He makes a useless grab, and it soars past him, smashing through the window with a massive tinkling of broken glass.

We watch the *Book of Light* speeding onward and upward into the evening sky.

'Why the hell did you do that?' he asks in a stunned voice.

I swallow. Something major is happening to the sky. Clouds are rushing towards each other, massing in huge stormy billows.

'I'm not sure,' I say nervously. 'I think – I thought it was maybe time we changed the rules.'

Everything goes black.

No stars, street lights, house lights, headlights, tail-lights on planes. They're all simply swallowed into a silent fathomless pitch-black infinity. It's like Martin and I are the only two beings left on a totally empty planet. It doesn't feel like a bad darkness. It just feels intensely electrically still.

This feeling of electric waiting builds to an unbearable pitch. High over the city something breaks open. There's a silent burst of light, as pure and absolute as the darkness that came before. Then indescribably sweet vibes come flooding down.

I see dread in Martin's eyes, mixed with terrible longing.

'No disrespect, man,' I say, 'but I think you're over.'

As the angelic vibes stream down into the city, they

take on shapes that make me think of shimmering letters from some unearthly alphabet.

They flutter in through the broken glass, settling in snowy mother-of-pearl drifts, and I know I'm looking at a pure form of the angelic information that has been inaccessible since medieval times.

A brisk breeze blows through the room. The symbols swirl across the floor and rise to form a dancing spiral, surrounding Martin with luminous encircling strands; then they close in.

For a moment I glimpse a stricken face peering out through all that unearthly light; not Martin's. Something disturbingly alien. Then with a tremendous *whoosh*, something funnels up through the ceiling and the thirteenth floor vanishes for ever.

I'm on a draughty stairway in Mortagaine House. The first thing I notice is the noise. Doors opening, footsteps and voices overhead, the sound of a radio, and what might be someone whizzing something up in a blender.

Beside me is a boy in eighties clothes.

Martin's ghost and I take a long thoughtful look at each other, long enough for me to know this is really who he is. He gives me a funny little grin, pulls a silvery yo-yo out of his back pocket and demonstrates a stunt my childhood friends and I used to call Walk the Dog.

I watch him for a few minutes. He's good. Surprisingly slick. Must have been putting in a lot of practice.

I hate to be disrespectful to a dead kid who's been through what Martin's been through, but there's something I've got to do.

'I've got to go,' I say gently. 'Walk me to the lift, if you want.'

Maybe he's absorbed with some new yo-yo trick, because halfway down the corridor he starts to lag behind.

I hear ghostly footsteps scuffle on the tiles, then they stop, and when I turn round the corridor is empty.

I don't know if there is some special dimension where they help troubled spirits get over the kind of nightmare that happened to Martin; if not there damn well ought to be.

Yet despite everything I have the feeling he's OK. I think that's why he appeared to me on the stairs, a kind of thank-you card, almost, so I'd know he appreciated what I'd done.

Also I think Martin wanted me to understand that wherever he hangs out now, life is unexpectedly cool. I like that. I like to think of him working up new yo-yo moves with his mates, doing crazy ten-year-old dares, maybe even happy, but most of all free.

I have no idea what time – or even what day – it is, out in the real world. But when I get outside Mortagaine House, it's a cold clear autumn evening and the only shadows have a source of light.

I hurry through brightly lit streets to the city hospital.

When my mother sees me, she falls into my arms. 'He's been on the operating table for five hours,' she sobs. 'They say we've got to prepare ourselves for the worst. He could die, Dino! Your dad could actually die.'

I never used to think that much about my mother, like I never really used to think about my old home. And like I used to believe suffering was something that only happens to people who somehow screw up. Now I'm wondering if maybe it's just how you know you're really human.

My mother is thirsty, but she's completely baffled by the vending machine, so I go and tinker with it for a while, systematically putting in coins and pressing buttons, and eventually hot coffee-coloured fluid spurts out.

I'm carefully lowering a scalding-hot plastic cup into Mum's hands, when a small white-haired woman bursts in through the door of the waiting room. 'Is he OK?' she sobs. 'Is Kostos going to be OK?'

She whips off her sunglasses and my mother gasps. 'Tippie! Oh, Tippie, you came!'

EPILOGUE

SADIE never talks about the time a dark angel tried to take her baby.

When I go round to her place, we do girl stuff, watch weepy chick flicks on DVD, flick through catalogues planning what outfits she'll buy when she gets back down to a size 10.

She dropped the flower fairy look after her baby was born. Sadie's a jeans girl these days, says it's easier to wash out the baby-goop. I think it's more that she's finally grown up.

Sadie and Dad split when Layla was three months old. To be fair to Dad, he didn't run out on them. The opposite in fact. He hung around pathetically for weeks, though it was humiliatingly obvious that his and Sadie's relationship was well and truly over.

When she finally, very firmly, asked him to leave, my father fell to bits. He took to phoning Mum all hours, begging for advice. 'But I've changed,

Claudette,' he wailed. 'Why can't she see I've changed? All I want is one last chance. One last chance of happiness.'

But where Sadie's concerned, my father has used up his final last chance and that's that.

'He does and says all these lovely caring things,' she told me once. 'But it's like he's just playing a part. The awful thing is, I don't think he knows there's a difference. Plus – oh, I don't know, Bee. I still love him, you know, but I don't trust him. Is that a terrible thing to say?'

I'm absolutely positive she did the right thing.

It's true that, thanks to Victor and the other dedicated people who helped him back on the road to recovery, my dad lives a relatively normal life. He *has* changed in some ways. He doesn't drink, he hardly ever gambles, and, as far as I know, he's not kept awake at nights by disturbing visions. The damage isn't anything you can see or touch. But he's been burned somewhere deep inside.

Tim gives off the same vibe. They're like convalescents who've just been released from hospital: light is too bright for them, the TV is too loud.

Not that we see Tim much these days. He's totally

stopped coming to the community centre. Victor is convinced, though, that Tim will make a full recovery.

'He's young. And he has that kind of pig-headed strength which will finally kick in when he gets older. Your dad, on the other hand . . .' He shook his head. 'Sorry, Bee.'

'It's not your fault,' I told him painfully.

He briefly touched my shoulder. 'No, but he's your dad and you love him.'

I do, despite everything. But, like Sadie, I don't trust him, not any more. James Molloy makes a great Saturday dad, but, like Mum always said, he's not a man for the long haul.

Victor Waverley, on the other hand, seems to be here to stay. He and Mum are so happy, it's embarrassing. He hasn't moved in or anything. They insist they both need their space; but he comes round so often he might as well.

I hang out with them sometimes, partly to be friendly, partly because, strange as it might seem, Victor is surprisingly good company. Some people would let this Guardian thing set them apart, but he's totally down-to-earth and normal, plus he has a wicked sense of humour.

'Think I'll ever meet my Mr Right?' Sadie asked me one time, as she bundled another load of baby clothes in the washing machine.

'Of course! He's out there. You've just got to find him, girl!'

'It's not just me,' she said wistfully. 'Layla is such a great kid. She deserves a dad who'll be there through thick and thin.'

When we aren't watching DVDs, or discussing strategies to find baby Layla a real dad, my dad's ex-girlfriend and I talk about little Miss Bossy Boots herself.

Like, is there any way to get her to eat a green vegetable which doesn't involve bribing her with chocolate buttons? And what in the world is this little human dynamo going to be like when she hits her teens, if she is this opinionated at one year old?

Even though Sadie and I are the best of friends these days, I never talk to her about Dino. To me that's private.

The other night he phoned just as I was falling asleep. No hello, just, 'What tune am I thinking of, Molloy?'

He was walking back from Zorba's in the rain.

287

He's been working for his uncle a few months now; his family needs the money.

Twelve months on, Dino's dad is still painfully frail. The doctors say the operation almost certainly worked, but for the time being Dino has to be the man of the house. He doesn't make a big deal out of it. He says he's just glad to have the old dinosaur back safe and sound.

What with my dance classes and Dino working three nights a week, we don't get much time together, but I'm determined not to be a whingeing high-maintenance girlfriend. I try to make the best of what time we have, but it's not always easy!

Like, last week, Dino and I were babysitting for Sadie. We were building towers out of wooden blocks for Layla to send smashing down, the way you do. Then Layla decided to build her own tower. When she finally managed to place one brick shakily on top of another, she was so proud she actually clapped herself, beaming all over her sticky little face. Then she immediately demolished it and started all over again.

It seemed as if she was happy amusing herself for a few minutes, so Dino stealthily put his arm around me.

Next minute my little sister was advancing on us with an outraged expression, yelling, 'Kiss, kiss, KISS!'

'Oh-oh. It's the kiss police,' I warned him. I explained that Layla automatically assumes all kisses have to be for her.

'Better pay the kiss tax then,' he grinned.

Dino swung Layla upside down, planting noisy kisses on her neck and tummy.

Out of the blue he said, 'I gave it to Victor, in the end.'

I knew he meant the yo-yo.

Dino gently set Layla down on her feet.

'Yeah,' he said huskily. 'I wanted Martin's family to have it, so they could have – what do they call that Oprah Winfrey thing?'

'Closure?' I suggested.

'But I couldn't just rock up to their house, and hand it over stone cold after twenty years. So Victor suggested we did it through proper police channels. Then after the parents had some time to get over the shock, he paid them a visit, told them we wanted to name the centre's recording studio after their son.'

'That is such a cool idea,' I said.

A few months ago, Dino shared the DJ spot at some big party down at the community centre. Afterwards Victor let Dino and some other boys talk him into converting an old storage room into a studio, where young wannabe DJs can improve their skills.

It's amazing how the hardest, meanest kids can change, once they get on the decks. You see who they really are – at least, who they *could* be, given a chance. I guess you could say the work of the Guardians is still going on, just in a different form.

A couple of nights after the Martin Coombs studio was officially opened, I dropped by on my way to babysit for Sadie. A skinny kid in a flying helmet whipped open the door, and started sshing me frantically. I heard this unbelievable voice coming from inside.

It was the famous song from *Souls for Sale*. But the way she sang it on the album was nothing compared to this. There was a new quality to Mimi's voice: raw, almost harsh, yet so tender too – as if she was comforting a little child in the night. She sang as if she couldn't care less if she was singing well or badly, she just wanted to draw out all the hurt and poison in the world and turn it into something –

maybe not beautiful, but real.

We stood, completely transfixed; me, Dino, the boys in their street clothes. Victor came to stand behind me in the doorway.

> *Each time the darkness comes back remember*
> *Nothing lasts.*
> *Nothing lasts, nothing lasts,*
> *Each time the darkness comes back remember*
> *Nothing ever lasts, it never lasts*
> *But everything, everything oh, everything,*
> *every single little thing . . . matters, oh*
> *how much, how much it matters.*

It was the way she sang that last line, as if life had suddenly become indescribably precious.

And for the first time I understood what those lyrics meant. That's because of what happened in the hospital.

When I saw Sadie's newborn daughter lying there all blue with the cord still attached, like some pale twisty root, I went numb. I just looked and looked and it was such a terrible sight, I was scared I'd go completely insane. My heart was bumping so hard, I thought it would explode right out of my chest. This baby was too unfinished to be a person. Most of all she was too still.

Sadie's face was all eyes, that's what I remember, those huge pleading eyes. She didn't even dare to ask what was wrong with her baby. She just whimpered like a wounded animal.

I wanted to run out of that hospital ward and keep on running and never ever go back. The only way I could force myself to stay in the delivery room was to physically grab on to Sadie.

In that moment everything changed. I completely forgot about how I was feeling. I just wanted to absorb some of Sadie's agony. I couldn't stand for her to feel this all by herself.

I felt a violent snapping sensation and part of me shot through into some completely different dimension.

I was still in the room in the hospital, watching the two midwives work frantically on that lifeless little body, but I was also with Dino.

I was there when he threw the *Book of Light* out through the window. I felt the explosion of energy as all that imprisoned power was finally released, shattering the evil spell of the thirteenth floor for ever.

Then I smashed back into the normal three-dimensional world of hospital smells and noises, just as the baby took a furious gulp of air. I saw this miraculous flicker of lightning go through her body, and next second she was pink and real; a living squirming bawling human baby.

We were all crying and laughing with relief, even the midwives.

'Now come and meet your mum,' the older woman crooned. 'Goodness, all that fuss you caused.'

She put the baby into Sadie's arms, still messy from being born, and both midwives agreed they'd never seen anything so perfect.

My little half-sister gripped on to my finger, staring into my face with wide misty-blue eyes.

I felt light-headed, literally dizzy, as if I'd been pulled back from some terrifying cliff edge I never knew existed. Now I'd always know it was there.

Sadie gazed besottedly at her little daughter, as if all her pain and terror were nothing compared to being able to hold this perfect little creature in her arms.

'What are you going to call her?' one of the midwives asked softly.

'Layla Bluebell Beatrice Rose,' Sadie said without hesitation.

I was horrified. 'Sadie! No *way*! That poor kid's going to have more initials than a satellite channel!'

It was so typical of that girl to give her baby four names when a normal person would settle for one or two. Next minute I threw my arms around her and cried because Sadie was naming her daughter after me.

'Will you look at that!' the older midwife said in a stunned voice.

Exquisite shapes fluttered past the window, melting against the glass.

'You must be a very special little girl, Layla Bluebell,' the young midwife crooned. 'It snowed on your birthday.'

The room slowly filled with a glimmering other-worldly radiance that I don't think I'll ever be able to describe.

The older midwife went around, snapping off overhead lights, then they went out, leaving us, still

clinging on to each other in the lamplight; so
exhausted and happy that the bed seemed to be
moving, like a raft sailing through a sea of shadows.